D0282704

The Curse
of the
Buttons

The Curse of the Buttons

ANNE YLVISAKER

CANDLEWICK PRESS

This is a work of fiction. Names, characters, places, and incidents are either
products of the author's imagination or, if real, are used fictitiously.

Copyright © 2014 by Anne Ylvisaker

All rights reserved. No part of this book may be reproduced, transmitted,
or stored in an information retrieval system in any form or by any means,
graphic, electronic, or mechanical, including photocopying, taping, and
recording, without prior written permission from the publisher.

First edition 2014

Library of Congress Catalog Card Number 2014931836
ISBN 978-0-7636-6138-0

14 15 16 17 18 19 BVG 10 9 8 7 6 5 4 3 2 1

Printed in Berryville, VA, U.S.A.

This book was typeset in Kennerly.

Candlewick Press
99 Dover Street
Somerville, Massachusetts 02144

visit us at www.candlewick.com

For my mother

Contents

Called Up

A wild howl tore through the night.

Ike snapped awake.

"Leon! Jim!" He thrashed his arms to roust his brothers, but the wide bed was empty.

He scrambled to the window. The howling went on, rising and falling like a wounded beast.

Steamboat.

Ike tucked his nightshirt into a pair of pants, grabbed his slingshot, and slipped down the stairs and out the back door.

All of Button Row was stirring. Father's snores sputtered, then stopped. LouLou and Jane called for Mother. A pan clattered next door, and next door to that, babies cried while Aunt Betsy shushed.

Barfoot whinnied in the lean-to. Ike ran to him and stroked his cheek. Across the alley, the Hinman dogs yowled along with the steamer whistle, and Mrs. Hinman hollered for Milton and Morris to just stay put.

Boats didn't arrive this late. They didn't wail this long. In the faint light of the half-moon, Ike climbed on Barfoot's back, urging him to gallop to the street, but Barfoot had only one gait.

Neighbors called out to neighbors. The new family from Kentucky staggered onto their porch in nightclothes. Farther on, Mr. Box threw open his bedroom window and waved his rifle.

"Have we been invaded, then?" he hollered.

"Don't know!" Ike shouted.

At Seventh, a light flickered in the

sanctuary window of Chatham Square Church.

"Wait here," Ike directed. He left Barfoot by the sycamore, dashed up the steps, and burst in.

The gust from the opening door extinguished the lone candle, but not before Ike saw Reverend Woolley and a colored man turn toward him in surprise.

"Isaac Button, what in tarnation?" thundered the Reverend. He relit the candle.

Ike stared. *Mr. Jenkins? At this church?* "I thought Albirdie might be—"

"My girl is in bed and so should you be. Get on, now."

"Yes, sir." Ike turned and stumbled out the door, down the steps, and smack into Albirdie Woolley.

"Come on," she whispered, grabbing his hand and tugging him toward the street. "It's something terrible or exciting or both."

Ike pulled away. "Where's Barfoot?"

"He's probably on his way home. We'll get there faster without him."

The steamer let loose one last long whistle. The silence it left was more urgent than its cry. Albirdie and Ike cut diagonally through yards and empty lots to the boardinghouse on Water Street, then picked their way down the slope to the shore, where a crowd was gathering.

The butter-and-egg man lumbered alongside his son, Junior. A motley band of drunks staggered forward, singing "Pop! Goes the Weasel." Ike and Albirdie darted around them. There stood Leon and Jim, hemmed in by Mr. Day, the grocer, and Mr. Day's slow-moving brothers.

"Why didn't you wake me?" Ike demanded, but before Leon and Jim could answer, Albirdie ducked between the men, and Ike and his brothers followed.

"Look!" she cried.

"It's the *Jeannie Deans*!" said Jim.

The boat hovered like the ghost of an enormous wedding cake just offshore. Acrid smoke filled the air. A man on board was hollering as deckhands built a gangway.

"What's news?" people kept shouting, so that no one could hear him.

"Quiet!" commanded the butter-and-egg man. The mob simmered, waiting.

The man hollered again. This time his message was passed person to person, and a cheer went up.

"The rebels are in Hannibal!" Leon shouted.

"Iowa's called up at last!" cried Jim.

"Iowa!" Ike cheered with the rest. "Iowa! Iowa! Iowa!" he yelled until he was hoarse.

Jim hooted and wrestled Leon to the ground. They sprang up and grabbed Ike and Albirdie and spun them around.

"So long, Keokuk!" Leon called, sweeping his arm toward town.

They followed as the throng marched up Main, dispersing to spread the news.

"Good riddance, OK Bakery!" Jim hollered.

"Been nice to know you, Hess Clothing!" Ike shouted. "Don't forget me, Gate City Carriage!"

Leon shoved Ike playfully. "What're you good-bying for?" he said. "You're eleven. You're not going anywhere."

Ike stopped. The butter-and-egg man bumped into him, knocking him to the ground.

"Apologies!" he boomed, pulling Ike to his feet and brushing him off. "Where's my boy? Junior! Wait for your old pa, now. Junior!"

Ike turned and ran to the shore. The steamer's whistle echoed in his head. The last whiff of smoke hovered in the still air. He listened to the deckhands call back and forth as they tramped along the gangway.

Leon was right.

All these months of waiting for Lincoln's call to the War Between the States, of watching men learn to be soldiers, parading up and down Main with rakes over their shoulders to stand in for rifles, of laughing at the surprise of soldiers from smaller towns who marveled at the splendor of Keokuk's four-story buildings and the twenty-five-foot flag at Day Bros. Grocery. All these months, the excitement of war had enveloped Keokuk, like a grand game everyone was in on.

And now his brothers would leave and take that excitement with them. His father and uncles and boy cousins, too.

Ike loaded his slingshot, pulled back, and sent the stone soaring into the lightening sky.

Albirdie came and stood by his side.

"That was a waste of a good rock," she said.

"I should be going with them."

Albirdie plucked out a small stone from the river and handed it to Ike. "But you're not," she said. "And neither am I."

Arduous Mayhem

"Eleven is not too young for war," Ike said to Barfoot, who swished his tail agreeably, then lumbered to the yard table and stuck his nose in an unattended pie. The family was milling about behind their attached houses, packing knapsacks and beginning their good-byes.

"Perfect aim. Watch!" said Ike. He held up his slingshot and pivoted slowly, scoping a worthy target: Father and uncles under the oak, inspecting packs; Leon and Jim rough-housing with boy cousins, little girls playing tag around them; lean-to stable; a rickety two-wheeled wagon. No.

"Perfect aim!" He continued revolving: strawberry bushes; green beans climbing tripod stakes; flowering sweet peas; rain barrel, full; woodpile, dwindling.

"Perfect aim!" Three gray houses, paint peeling. One wide connecting porch, sagging. Aunties with armloads of folded shirts and pants banging in and out of two screen doors, while Mother leaned against a third, hankie to her eyes.

And past that third door, the oak again. The men. And above their heads, a nest; a papery wasp nest dangling from the lowest branch. Inside, a buzzing army awaiting orders.

Ike set his feet wide and drew back the stone.

"Fire!" he cried, and everyone ducked.

He released the missile.

It sailed over the yard table, over Barfoot's head, past brothers and sisters and cousins. Then it grazed Uncle Hugh's head, smacked into the tree trunk, and dropped into an open knapsack. A lone wasp buzzed over the gathering before flying in an open window.

"Enough nonsense, Isaac!" Father boomed. "Olive, we need another shirt over here for Jim."

Ike stuck his slingshot in his waistband and pulled Barfoot from the pie. "A breeze took it," he muttered. "And perfect aim is not nonsense." The swaybacked pony nickered and smeared his strawberry snout across Cousin Susannah's back.

"Barfoot," she said, wiping his nose with her apron, then feeding him a lump of sugar. "You old fool."

"Gather 'round," Uncle Hugh bellowed, his brothers Oscar and Dan joining him on the wide back porch. "Soldier sons, our dear wives, darling daughters."

"And Ike!" Ike hollered.

"Hush!" said Father.

"And Ike," Ike mumbled to Barfoot.

"An occasion such as this brings to mind

all the great sojourns of the Button clan," Uncle Hugh began. "We remember California's rivers of gold, and subsequent successes there, affording the fineries we enjoy within them there walls."

Ike nudged Susannah. "California."

Susannah shrugged. "We all know it was Uncle Palmer, rest his long-gone soul, went to California and got the gold. And look at this dress. Finery? I think not."

Uncle Oscar gave his daughter Susannah a look. "There was the great traverse from the east," he said. "The arduous trail of adventure and mayhem that brought the Button brothers to the banks of the Mississippi River and settlementation in Keokuk, Ioway."

"I could traverse arduous mayhem," Ike whispered to Susannah.

Susannah shook her head. "No you couldn't. Besides, it was only Illinois, and Mother says they were stranded here because their horses were stolen and only Palmer had the fortitude to continue."

"Even so," he said too loudly, "from the east!"

"Quiet!" said Father.

"And now," Ike's father continued, "on this momentous day of June, eighteenhundred-andsixtyone, after weeks of drills and military activities within the gentle arms of our beloved city, we and our sons tomorrow depart these shores. We will venture south, on commission of Governor Kirkwood, to preserve the union of these United States for our children, and our children's children, and so forth and so on, just as Lincoln has called us to do."

Soldier sons cheered, piling onto the porch and beating their drumsticks on the rail.

Ike was surrounded by little girls clapping and squealing, while aunties bounced screaming babies. Mother sat at the yard table weeping while Susannah patted her back.

"They could be maimed!" Mother wailed. "Or *killed*!"

And up on the porch, the Button men. Not tall, but sturdy, and smartly dressed, with silky mustaches and hair sharply parted and greased. They stepped back and gathered their sons around them. The boys seemed to swell in size up there in front of the family. His family. His father and brothers. His uncles and cousins. Iowa First, Union army. Ike ached with pride. He should be on that porch, too.

"To war, men!" Father declared.

"To war!" Ike cried, starting toward them, but Mother nabbed his shirt and held him back.

"A song! Lead us in a farewell song, Susannah!" Uncle Oscar said, beckoning her to the step.

Susannah grabbed Ike's arm.

"'America,'" she said to him. "Sing it

14

slow and maybe they'll be satisfied with just one."

Ike glanced over his shoulder at the men, then out at the women and girls.

"My country, 'tis of thee," they started, but on two different notes. They stopped and Susannah hummed a note to Ike and began again. She sang loud, he mouthed the words, and the family joined in, loud and off-key. Barfoot dipped his head and whinnied along.

Not Mustered

Ike lay awake between Leon and Jim, who were arguing loudly over the affections of dashing Kate from Kentucky. A mosquito buzzed overhead and Ike swatted at the air, then scratched at the bites on his ankle.

"She intended that photograph for my pocket, and you looked the fool snatching it from her hand," Leon said to Jim.

"One look at your sour face and she would have run had I not been there to accept her sweet offering with the dignity of a departing hero," said Jim.

"Departing hero?" scoffed Leon. "Caught a lot of rebels with that drum, have you?"

"Many as you," said Jim.

"Quietyou'llwakeyourmother!" came the voice of their father through the window. He and the uncles were at the yard table, talking in low voices.

Leon and Jim went silent, but Jim reached over Ike and socked Leon. Leon smacked back. Ike sat up between them to block further attack.

His brothers seemed older. They'd had their leaving baths, so the sweat and straw smell was washed off them, and Uncle Hugh had trimmed their hair. Jim had had to pack two of Father's shirts because his shoulders popped the seams of his own. Leon had fuzz over his lip and his voice was deepening.

Ike put his hand to his own lip. Smooth as the edge of a penny.

"I want to go with you," he said.

"You're not mustered," said Leon.

"The *Jeannie Deans* is big enough for one more man," said Ike.

"Man!" Jim laughed. "You're not going, remember, because you're eleven. Man!"

17

Ike moved to the foot of the bed. "You're not men, either," he said. "You don't even have guns. Drums. I could manage a drum as well as either of you."

"You didn't seem too eager to manage a drum when we were waking up for drill at four and a half every morning," said Leon.

"But that was just here in Keokuk. Everyone said it would be over before you got called up."

"Everyone was wrong," said Jim. "And you're not trained."

"You can teach me," said Ike.

"You don't have a drum," said Leon.

"I have drumsticks."

"Twigs," said Jim. "Not actual drumsticks."

"What if you get lost?" said Ike. "I'm good with directions."

"How could we get lost?" said Leon. "We'll be with the whole company."

"Besides," said Jim, "the river goes south. Can't get lost next to the river."

"Do you have a map?" said Ike. "Albirdie says in the South you can't depend on the river."

"What does your girlfriend know about the South?" said Leon.

"Albirdie is not my girlfriend. And she does know."

"She knows cheating is what she knows," said Jim.

Leon laughed. "Poor Jim. Bested by a twelve-year-old checkers fiend."

Jim kicked Ike aside and wedged Leon's head into the crook of his elbow.

"I could carry your drum," said Ike, helping Leon pull free. "I could set up your tent."

"Forget it," said Jim.

"We got no say in it," said Leon, clapping a mosquito between his palms. "You're too young. You can't go."

"But what if—"

"Stop, Ike!" said Jim. "Let us enjoy our last night on a real bed."

"But I—"

"Quietyou'llwakeMother," Leon and Jim muttered. They rolled their backs away from Ike, and within a few lengthening breaths they were snoring.

Ike stood on the bed, stepped over Jim, and jumped to the floor. He went to the window.

Three cigar tips glowed in the dark. Bottles clinked. The familiar rhythm of the men's nightly banter rose and fell. Ike rested his elbows on the sill and leaned out to listen.

Out of Reach

". . . is nearly gone. All of it."

Ike breathed in the swirl of smoke that drifted up into the warm night, savoring the low rumble of the men's voices. *Gone? What's gone?*

"The money was Palmer's, anyhow. He would have wanted us to live well, all the trouble he went to."

"Living well's done, brothers. Captain Hinman put a notice in today's paper: *You and each of you are hereby notified* and such and so."

"Never mind Hinman. He just never had faith in the possibility. And he's on the river more than home."

"Hinman won't throw 'em out while we're away. A fellow what's defending his country, that's a man people respect."

Throw them out? Them who?

"He's right. We'll come back respectable and start up a proper business. Likely we've loafed long enough."

"Indeed. All this war talk has got me stirred up with ambition. This time I'll get me a nice little shack and shod horses."

"I'm thinking a saloon. *Button Bros.* Fancy the business heroes bring in. I wonder how much it'd take. I wonder—"

"Details, details. You boys sound like Palmer, all your *I wonder* this and *What if* that. Never letting up. It's no use, I tell you."

"He's right. It's always turned out before."

"What I mean is, there's no point in making plans. Losing Palmer was a curse upon us. There ain't no way for a Button to distinguish hisself without Palmer."

"Palmer," said Uncle Hugh. "Wily old

Palmer. The lot of us mudheads, and him taking aim and firing true."

"Palmer," said Uncle Oscar, laughing. "Truth is, we could use us a Palmer right now."

"Point us in the right direction," said Father.

"If he were going with us —"

"I hear you, brother."

The men sighed.

"Ah, Palmer!" The bottles clinked again and there was a long silence, followed by a single belch.

Ike stood up and bumped his head on the window sash.

"What was that?"

"Just a noise. Calm yourself, man. There's more than noises where we're going."

"Enough of this talk. Big day tomorrow. Go on, brothers."

The men snuffed out their cigars and said their good-nights.

Ike stood just inside the window until he heard the back door click shut.

Pockets Bulging

Ike waited until he heard his father tromp up the steps and close the door across the hall, then he went to his shelf and studied it in the moonlight:

- six open mollusks, one grasping a pearl
- a crock holding twenty-seven marbles
- two towers of wooden checkers—twelve red and twelve black
- a cloth checkers mat, rolled up
- three Indian arrowheads
- a picture card of the president
- two sturdy twigs, roughly whittled into short drumsticks
- a slingshot and two stones

- a small carved bear from California
- a photograph of the Button men

If he were going with us . . .

They meant Palmer, of course. But why not Ike, who was right here? *If Ike were going with us . . .*

. . . taking aim, firing true, direction . . . Hadn't he just today shown them his perfect aim? Couldn't he point the way?

Ike took the photograph to the window. He could barely make it out, but he knew the details by heart. They were younger, thinner. All four had cigars in their mouths. Three wore bow ties.

First was his father, seated, with the fullest mustache obscuring his mouth.

To his left was Hugh, high forehead, narrow mustache, nearly a smile.

Oscar stood behind them, solemn, eyebrows and mustache drooping like his mouth.

Then Palmer. Not younger by much, but

25

fairer, leaning forward, just a wisp of upper-lip hair, cigar dangling out of the middle of his mouth. Straight tie.

If he were going with us. If Ike were going with us.

Ike set the picture down and fingered the California bear. He didn't remember his dead uncle, but he'd imagined him plenty. An adventurer. Probably with a swift horse and a worn map. Pockets bulging with gold. A rifle. Perfect aim—like Ike. Good with directions—like Ike. If Palmer could go to California by himself, surely Ike could go south in the company of the Button men.

Ike rearranged the shelf, putting to one side a leaving collection, things he would take if he *were* going, considering economy of space as well as potential situations:

- the slingshot but not the stones, which could be found along the way
- the sharpest of the arrowheads, though a pocketknife would be even better

- one of the mollusks — it could be handy as a spoon or for digging
- the newly whittled drumsticks
- the bear for luck

He could earn his keep, besides, with some gaming. Marbles or checkers? He was better at checkers, but marbles were easier to pocket. He took five muddies and a taw from the crock and placed them in front of the bear, but they rolled off the slightly slanted shelf and clattered to the floor.

Ike dove to sweep them up and crouched there, still, listening for his brothers, who would not be pleased to be awakened. But they simply suspended their breathing mid-snore, then in unison began again, shallow at first, then deep and hearty.

The mollusk could go in a shirt pocket, slingshot and drumsticks in his waistband, and everything else in pants pockets.

He picked up a stack of checkers, then set them back.

Checkers made him think about winning and losing. Losing made him think about Albirdie Woolley. She had cleared every boy and girl who dared challenge her of each token they anted. Even Jim. She used Ike for practice, and they played countless games in the back pew of her father's church while listening to the various speeches and political carryings-on that took place there, so Ike felt some pride in her accomplishments.

Last week Albirdie had won an official army compass off an unsuspecting soldier who came to her father's church for a strengthening prayer.

Direction . . . He could find his way anywhere in Keokuk, but he'd never had to test his inner compass outside town. Could he really find his way in the South?

Ike got to thinking about the mysterious force that pulled the compass's small arrow. He thought about the words *north* and *south* in the way he'd heard them bandied about these last months. Keokuk rode the very coattails of *north,* but though *south* was as near as Missouri, he had never been there. None of them had, as far as Ike knew. Not even Palmer.

Ike needed Albirdie's official compass.

He dressed quickly, plucked Lincoln from the shelf, and the mollusk with the pearl, then snuck down the stairs and out the back door.

The Bear and the Compass

The crickets were putting up a racket that covered Ike's nighttime movements, and Barfoot snorted sleepily in the livery. Ike rubbed his horse's neck.

"Come on, boy, wake up," he said. "Let's go see Albirdie."

He swung himself onto Barfoot's back, coaxing him down the alley and into the street. It would be faster on foot, but this could be their last ride together for a while. They clopped down Morgan, across Seventh, to the church. Albirdie and her father had quarters at the back.

"Don't wander far," Ike whispered.

He climbed the sycamore and edged toward the middle window. He whistled three short notes and a long one. He waited, then whistled again. A moment later the door below him creaked open and a candlelit figure waved him in.

The air in the sanctuary was stale and cool. In the moonlight, the pulpit loomed like a hovering ghost and the altar cross stood at dark attention. Ike slid into the back pew next to Albirdie. She'd pulled a dress on over her nightgown, and she fidgeted with the sleeves. "What is it?" she asked.

"Rematch," he said, pulling the mollusk from his pocket.

"You woke me up for a rematch? I thought something exciting was happening." She stood. "I can beat you at checkers tomorrow."

"Wait." Ike spit on his index finger, polished the pearl, and held it up close to her face. Albirdie reached for it, but Ike cupped his hand around the shell.

31

"If I win, I get your compass," he said.

"No," she said. She pulled a brass button from the hymnal box on the back of the pew, the place where she stored her things. "This might be from the uniform of a general."

"It has to be the compass."

"No."

Ike glanced up at the pulpit, then looked down at his bare feet.

"It's for my brothers," he said. "A traverse such as theirs . . ."

"You wouldn't give up that pearl for your brothers."

"*As Lincoln has called . . .*" Ike started again, but at the sound of footfalls he ducked to the floor.

Albirdie pinched out the flame between her thumb and index finger, then dropped the kneeling rail and lowered herself onto it, folding her hands on the pew in front of her.

"Albirdie Ilene!" Ike heard the Reverend

exclaim. "What in heaven's name are you doing in here?"

"The Iowa First is leaving tomorrow," she said calmly. "You said we should pray for their safety."

"Well, now," said Reverend Woolley. "So I did. So I did. Be quick about it, then, and back to bed."

"Yes, Father."

They were quiet for a long moment, then Albirdie raised the kneeler and kicked Ike.

"All clear."

Ike set the mollusk next to Albirdie.

"I need the compass," he said.

"There's not time for a whole game now. He'll be back to check on me."

"Then trade me the pearl for the compass."

"Why?"

Ike opened his mouth and closed it. *For my shelf. For my leaving collection. So I can . . .*

Albirdie got up to go.

33

"What if I went with them?" Ike blurted. "South. I'd need to find my way."

Albirdie sat down again. She did not say *You're too young* or *That's foolish*.

"It's not the getting lost you got to worry about," she said.

"Still." Ike set Lincoln next to the mollusk. "The compass would help."

"There's plenty of important things to do here," said Albirdie.

"No," said Ike. "The men are going south. I want to go with them."

Albirdie propped the Lincoln card on her lap. She fingered the shell.

"The pearl is a pretty thing," said Ike.

"It's small," said Albirdie. She handed it back to him.

"But gleaming." Ike held it up to her face. "It's a rare treasure from the Mississippi. Even Leon has tried to talk me out of this pearl."

Albirdie set the picture down and took the shell from him again.

"And your California bear," she said.

Besides the photo of the Button men, the bear was Ike's one tangible piece of evidence that Palmer had existed and that he'd gotten all the way to California. He felt Palmer's strength when he held it.

"No. Lincoln and the pearl. But not the bear."

"Then you'll have to go without the compass."

"Fine. I will." Ike grabbed Lincoln and the mollusk and stomped to the door.

"Wait. I really like that bear." Albirdie followed him to the door. "Think about the bear. I'll bring the compass to the *Jeannie Deans* tomorrow just in case. Come to the gangway."

Gone

There was threat of rain. There were flocks of hankies waving. There were tears and shouts and swelling cheers as soldiers passed in ragged lines through the mass of Keokukians to their waiting steamboat. The ground vibrated with the feet of a thousand men.

Ike stood wedged between Susannah and his mother, straining to see the Buttons pass by. How could there be this many men in all of Iowa, much less on one levee? How would the *Jeannie Deans* carry them all?

His plan was to walk alongside the Button men when they passed, gradually slipping into the ranks behind them. Few of the soldiers wore uniforms, only their packs and jubilation distinguishing them from civilians. He touched each of his filled pockets and checked the slingshot and sticks tucked into his waistband.

It had seemed like a good plan in the familiar confines of his room, but a small bulb of doubt had sprouted in his chest as they'd approached the levee, and with every wave of soldiers, it grew, squeezing his breath into short, tight gasps. He took out the bear and held it hard in one hand. He would find Albirdie. He would trade the California bear for the compass.

"Ike!"

"Leon!"

"Help me out, will you?" Leon pulled Ike into line with him.

Ike's heart swelled and he breathed in, stumbling as he tried to stay next to Leon in the crush of arms and legs and heaving chests. Leon *did* want him along! Ike imagined the weight of a drum hanging from his shoulders. He saw himself deep in the woods — holding his compass in front of him, leading his brothers to . . . And there the scene stopped. *What would they encounter in the South? Fort Sumter had burned. Would they be surrounded by fire? Would they see dead men? Would rebels put spears through their stomachs?*

No matter. He was going.

"Yes! Anything!"

"Good," said Leon. "Kate was supposed to be here. I can't find her. Give her this note." He stuffed a small, folded paper into Ike's hand, gave Ike's shoulders a quick squeeze, then pushed him back into the sea of spectators.

"Good-bye, brother!" Leon called, marching on.

"Wait!" Ike hollered. "Leon!" He shoved the note deep into his pocket and pushed his way back into the ranks. "Leon! Wait!"

Albirdie had said she'd be here; all he had to do was find Albirdie. Then he'd catch up to Leon. He let lines of men pass him so he could be sure to see Albirdie at the gangway.

The last of the soldiers were boarding. Deckhands were lifting the thick securing ropes. And there! There was the Reverend, spreading his arms out to bless every man he could reach, Albirdie by his side.

Ike waved the bear over his head, trying to catch Albirdie's eye. The *Jeannie Deans* let out three short whistles, and all of Keokuk broke into song.

"Ain't that a fine trinket," barked a deep voice behind him, and the bear was snatched from Ike's hand. He whirled around, dukes up for a fight, but he was looking into the wide midsection of a uniformed giant.

"You can drop them china teacups and step aside," said the stranger, leaning his smirking face into Ike's. "Go home and wait for the blessings sure to rain down on you for the gift you give your country." He laughed and kissed the bear, then popped it in his chest pocket and shoved Ike out of line.

"Hey! Give it back!" Ike lunged for the bear but was swallowed by the singing crowd and lost his bearings. Which way was the river? Where was the steamer? Where was Albirdie? He could feel the imprint of the bear on his palm where he'd been clutching it. He opened his sweaty fist and looked at his empty hand.

"Leon! Albirdie!" Ike's voice evaporated in the cacophony of the crowd. He followed the mournful cry of the steamer whistle and pushed his way to the shore just as the *Jeannie Deans* pulled away.

"Wait!" he hollered.

It was moving so slowly. He could still reach it.

He waded into the river.

"Father!" He didn't notice his sopping pants. "Don't leave me here!"

"Leon! Jim!" He was up to his waist and the current snapped at his legs.

"Uncle Hugh! Uncle Oscar! Wait!"

The boat turned, heading south, the soldiers growing smaller. Then it passed Mud Island and drifted out of sight.

"Stop!"

Ike's voice faltered. He stood staring at the wide Mississippi, Keokuk's road to Hannibal . . . St. Louis, New Orleans . . . the Gulf of Mexico. He slapped the water with his empty hands. "Wait!"

"I said to meet me at the gangway."

Albirdie. It was drizzling now, and her hair sprang out in curls.

The hubbub faded as those left behind returned to their homes and businesses.

"If you'd given me the compass last night, I'd be on the boat now," Ike yelled, wading to shore.

Albirdie held up the compass, which was hanging on a string around her neck. "If you'd come to the boat, I would have."

Ike reached for the compass, but she held it to her chest.

41

"I did! I did come to the boat!"

"Do you have the bear, then?"

He looked at her hard. "No."

She shrugged. "I didn't think you'd give it up."

Ike pulled the handful of marbles from his pocket and threw them into the river. There was no use explaining. One by one he whipped his whittled drumsticks away, too. He turned and stomped off, then broke into a run. He glanced back and saw Albirdie following, but he didn't wait for her to catch up.

Alone

Ike fell out of bed with a thud. No brothers. The sun was already halfway across the floor. His stomach rumbled. It all came back to him: the crush of soldiers, the *Jeannie Deans,* his brothers, the giant and the bear. Gone. The Iowa First would be in Hannibal by now.

He slouched into his clothes and stood at his shelf, taking stock. Lincoln, Palmer and the men, checkers, mat, marbles, arrow-heads, slingshot, mussels, stones. A half-eaten beef stick. Why had he thrown his drumsticks in the river? He gnawed a bite off the beef stick and touched the place the bear should be. A crush of self-pity settled on his chest.

Downstairs, next door, and next door to that—all women and girls. Leon had pulled him into the ranks, then pushed him away. It was Leon's fault that Palmer's bear was gone. That Ike missed Albirdie and the compass. He would be in Hannibal, too, if it weren't for Leon. This wouldn't have happened to Palmer.

Downstairs, the shades were drawn against the light and Mother lay on the sofa with a damp washrag over her face. LouLou and Jane were nestled into Father's chair, whispering and playing paper dolls.

"Shhh!" they hissed, pointing at Mother.

"But—" Ike started.

"Shhh!" they hissed again.

Next door, Aunt Sue was sorting strawberries.

"What am I going to do with all these berries piling up and no men to eat them?" she demanded. She shook her head at Ike and dropped a handful onto the table, motioning for him to sit in Uncle Oscar's chair.

"Do your part," she said.

Ike ate obediently, keeping his eyes on the table.

"My husband and sons — all gone. Least your mother still has you."

Ike stuffed the last strawberry in his mouth and got up to leave.

"You're not full yet." She dumped another heap of berries in front of him.

She nodded at the *Gate City* spread open on the table.

"A shooting at *Day Bros. Grocery* in broad daylight. More soldiers coming to town, bringing us to ruin. I say keep them out at camp and away from decent folk. Why build a brand-new soldiering camp one mile north of town if you can't keep all the soldiers in it?"

Their men were soldiers; weren't the Button men decent folk? Ike pulled the paper toward him and read the story for himself. Mr. Grainger, excited by liquor, a pepperbox pistol, a reeling blow.

"Don't worry your mother today, or you'll be in the soup, understand? And keep the newspaper away from her. The news of late's been enough to curdle a soul even as stout as my own, and now, with the men soldiering? Fold it up, why don't you, and toss it in with Barfoot's messes."

"Where's Susannah?" Ike ventured, grasping for an excuse to escape.

"Next door," she said. "Helping with the babies. Keeps her mind off that boy she's pining over. Quit moping after those brothers, Ike. It's not as though they paid you any mind when they were here. Time you find something useful to do, like my Susannah."

Ike folded the newspaper and edged toward the door as Aunt Sue kept on.

"I says to her, I says, *Last thing we need*

is for you to be taking up with Thomas Britton.
He's a regular Palmer, that one. Just you look out."

Ike stopped. "How is he a regular Palmer?"

"And do you know what she says to me?" Aunt Sue continued, ignoring him. "She says, *Leastways Palmer*—"

"How is Thomas like Palmer?" Ike interrupted.

"Palmer!" she said sharply. "Pshaw. Going adventuring, leaving responsibility and heartbreak in his wake."

"But the gold," Ike said.

"Gold?" she scoffed. "The little pittance he sent back ain't a mite of what drowned with him, leaving us in debt to the Captain. Bold? I'll give the man that. Handsome? Oh, *my*, yes. But Palmer Button hain't the sense of a horsefly.

"Now, go over to Aunt Betsy's. Why, if I don't—"

Ike ducked out and went next door.

"Good morning, sleepyhead!" Aunt Betsy gathered him in a pillowy embrace, squashing one of the babies between them. "We've et, but bless your tired little heart, you slept right on through. We saved you plenty. Plenty! I know how to feed a growing boy, though the Lord saw fit to give me none of my own. No. Not a one. Just this whole passel of lassies."

Ike pulled away and the little girls giggled uncontrollably at the sight of a boy in their kitchen at this hour.

"They're a nuisance," Susannah said, handing Ike the other baby. He bounced her on his hip while Susannah peeled an egg for him and uncovered a plate of biscuits.

He handed the baby back, took two biscuits with a mumbled thank-you, and went out to the lean-to, where Barfoot waited patiently.

Ike fed Barfoot one of the biscuits, then sat on a straw bale.

They chewed in silence, listening to

Goldenrod and Marigold barking over at the Hinmans', and old man Hinman yelling at them to stop. They heard Mrs. Hinman scold her father for taking a tone with the dogs. Goldenrod and Marigold stopped barking just long enough to eat whatever treats Mrs. Hinman must have given them, then they started in again.

Ike unfolded the newspaper and read the shooting story to Barfoot and one about a colt born without forelegs.

"Look at this flag." Ike flashed the paper at Barfoot. *"Our flag is there! And the star-spangled banner in triumph shall wave . . ."* he read. "Leon and Jim are there with the flag while we're here with these thrilling announcements: *Of river news there is scarcely anything to report. The Hawkeye State will pass up this morning. The river is falling fast.* A confidence man's been caught in Davenport. Lewis Sister shot a secessionist in Stewartville. Ohmer's Saloon has ice cream every day and evening. Tewksbury's celebrated strawberries are for sale at Louis Eck's saloon. I couldn't celebrate another strawberry if it were wearing a feathered cap."

Ike grabbed a brush from the tackle bucket and pulled it down Barfoot's coat, starting at his neck.

"You'll be in the soup," he said, mimicking Aunt Sue's shrill voice.

He worked his way down Barfoot's right side. "Think Palmer stayed out of the soup?" he said. "No."

He moved to Barfoot's left side and started brushing at his neck, working his way back again. "*Sense of a horsefly.* What does she know?"

Ike exchanged the brush for a wide-toothed currycomb and started working the snarls out of Barfoot's tail. "I am left behind."

Ike shook his head and kept working the coarse hairs. "You've got pie in here!"

He smoothed Barfoot's tail with his hands. "Think Palmer would have sat around eating strawberries with the women?"

He patted his horse's flank. "There. That's better. You look smart enough for a parade."

Barfoot whinnied.

"Calm down, pal. It's just an expression."

Barfoot whinnied again and stamped his hooves.

"Barfoot!" Ike scolded.

"Hi, Barfoot." It was Albirdie, wearing her infernal compass. She fed the horse a carrot. Ike ignored her and nudged Barfoot's head toward him. He reached for a handful of oats and held it out to Barfoot.

"I kept my word, if that's what you're mad about," Albirdie said. She held out another carrot. Barfoot nuzzled her hand, then her pocket, looking for more.

"It's not my fault you aren't in Hannibal with your brothers." She held up the compass, turning until she was facing south, and pointed.

Ike pulled Barfoot's head back again and brushed his snout.

"Go ahead and blame me if you want," she continued. "I'm going to the levee. All those people yesterday, the soldiers leaving? A person gets there early, they could find lots of things dropped and left behind." She kissed Barfoot's cheek and walked out to the alley. "Want to come?"

"Nope," said Ike.

"Fine. You'll have to win any treasures I scavenge, then. And that's not likely."

Ike continued brushing Barfoot until Albirdie was gone. Treasures. There *had* been a lot of people. He went to the alley and watched Albirdie break into a run.

"Shoot. There could be something useful at the levee." He hesitated, then climbed on Barfoot's back.

"Come on, Barfoot. We may as well give her a ride."

Scavenge

Main Street was as familiar to Ike as the terrain of his own room. He knew where the hooligans congregated after dark, which shopkeepers were feuding, and where he'd be most likely to get an apple or a lump of sugar for Barfoot. He kept Barfoot close to the sidewalk, letting faster horses and carriages pass in the middle.

These last months had transformed the usually placid city center into a hub of military preparation. Out-of-town carts and carriages bustled by, always in a hurry. Men shouted. Shop help kept broomsticks busy. Newcomers crossed the street in the middle of the block, gaping at the tall buildings. Ike and Albirdie let Barfoot edge over to Day Bros. Grocery, where he stopped in the shade of their awning.

A tall brown horse galloped past, pulling a boxy cart. Two faces peered out from under a pile of straw. Milton and Morris Hinman, hitching a ride.

"It'll be dark before you get anywhere, rate that old nag is going!" one of the boys hollered.

"He's a he!" Ike called after them, but the boys were already far ahead.

"Don't let Milton and Morris outrun us, Barfoot!" Albirdie shouted. She encouraged Barfoot with her heels, but he wouldn't budge.

"He's spooked," said Ike.

Mr. Day limped out with an apple for Barfoot. "Leave the poor boy here," he said. "The activity's too much for him."

"Thanks, Mr. Day," Ike said.

They walked the last blocks to the levee

and surveyed the ground. It was still damp, and anything left was muddy. Junior was there, too, with a sack hanging empty at his side.

"Look what I found," he said, holding up a torn bill. "Wisconsin money."

"Milton and Morris are over there. Look," said Albirdie.

"Hide your valuables," said Junior, tucking the bill in his pocket.

"Don't let on that I've got my compass," said Albirdie. She took it from around her neck and put it in her pinafore pocket.

"Hinmans," Ike scoffed. "Never mind the Hinmans. We'll just stay over on this section."

They walked slowly, side by side, scanning the ground.

"A spoon," said Ike. He held it up triumphantly, then put it in his shirt pocket.

"I'm hoping for some bullets," said Junior.

"Or Iowa money," said Albirdie. She picked up a blue knitted sock. "Perfect." She slipped her compass inside and stuck it back in her pocket.

"Ike! Junior! Albirdie!" Milton saw them and ran over. "Look here. A drumstick. Could have been Leon's or Jim's, Ike. What did you find? I'll trade you this genuine drumstick for it."

Ike reached for the drumstick. Milton pulled it back.

"Paws off, Button. Now, who wants it?"

Ike looked out at the river. Leon and Jim were out there somewhere. And his whittled drumsticks.

"You don't know what we have to trade yet," Junior pointed out.

Milton held the drumstick for Junior to inspect. Genuine.

Ike grabbed for it. "Give it to me. If it's Leon's or Jim's it belongs to me." Milton snatched it back, ignoring Ike.

"OK, then, Junior, I'll play you for it," said Milton. "Marbles. Double or nothing. I bet you found something good, didn't you?"

He reached for Junior's sack, but Junior held it close.

"Forget it," said Junior.

But Ike considered. His spoon was a good find, but an actual drumstick. If he got another one . . . Maybe he could still find a way south.

"All right," said Ike. He pulled out the spoon.

"Ike!" said Junior. "He's sly."

"Nice," said Milton, ignoring Junior and examining the spoon. "Silver. Bet I can get some money for that. He flashed a deck of worn cards. "Pick a card. Any card."

"I thought we were going to play marbles," said Ike.

"We would, but I don't have any on me. Do you?" said Milton.

"Nope. Junior? Albirdie?" They shook their heads.

"Come on. You've got a good chance of winning." Milton fanned out the deck. "Pick a card, any card."

"Don't do it, Ike," said Albirdie. "You're just going to lose that spoon."

"Are you going to listen to her or to your own good sense?" said Milton. Ike reached out his hand, then hesitated. Albirdie could be right. But then, he'd only had the spoon a few minutes, anyhow.

"It's an army drumstick," he said to Albirdie as he plucked a card from the middle of the deck. Jack of clubs. He showed it to Junior and Albirdie.

"Remember your card," said Milton. "Now. Put it here." He tapped the top of the deck. Then he cut the deck and restacked the cards. He cut it again. "I'm going to find your card. And if I can't, you get the drum-stick. Fifty-one chances for you; one chance for me."

Milton knelt and started flipping cards over, one by one. They huddled around him. He paused a couple of times, feeling the top card and looking into the distance, then continuing to turn over card after card, studying each one. Finally, he stopped, his hand hovering over the next unrevealed card. "Mmmm . . . mmhmmm. Can you feel that?" He held the deck out to them. Ike and Junior held their hand over it and shook their heads. Albirdie reached out, then pulled her hand back.

"It's a trick, Ike," she said.

Milton slowly drew the card up to face Ike.

"That's it!" Ike said, both thrilled and disappointed.

"Sorry, Ike." Milton grabbed the spoon from Ike's pocket. He held it with the drumstick. "Albirdie. What do you say? I'll play you for whatever you have in your pocket."

Albirdie pulled the compass from the sock in her pocket, held it up for Milton to see, then hung it around her neck. "Nope," she said. "You're a cheat."

Milton whistled at the sight of the compass. "Direct. Can't argue with direct." He glanced over at Morris, who gave him a wave and came to join them, lugging a bulging sack.

"I think we're done here," Morris said. "What did he swindle you out of, Ike?"

"Swindle?" said Milton. "We played cards, fair and square, didn't we, Ike? He's a wily one, our Ike. No, it was close. I edged him out this time, but next time, no telling."

They turned to leave but Milton came back.

"Hey, Albirdie. There were some men over at the junkyard saying your father's friendly with the coloreds. Is it true?"

They all looked at Albirdie. Ike remembered seeing Mr. Jenkins at the church and felt himself turning red without knowing why.

"So what if he is?" she said.

"Don't matter," said Milton. "Long as they're free. There's bounty on fugitives. A fellow could pick up some nice reward money if they're fugitives."

"And a fellow could get arrested if he

helps them," added Morris. "What would you do if your daddy was in jail?"

"Why don't you give us that compass, Albirdie, and we'll keep it quiet about your pa," said Milton.

"Shut up about my father. Iowa's a Free State," Albirdie said, putting her hand over the compass. "And pretty soon the whole country will be, too."

"Don't count on it," said Morris. He took the spoon from Milton and dropped it in the bag as they hurried over to another clump of kids. Milton held out the drumstick while Morris started scavenging around them.

"They make me so mad," said Albirdie. "Preying on innocent people with their lousy tricks. Building up trouble when they don't know a thing about anything."

"You've been had, Ike," Junior interrupted. "Look."

"What?" said Ike.

"They did it on purpose."

"What?" said Albirdie.

"The drumstick was a distraction. Morris cleaned up while we weren't looking."

Sure enough. There wasn't a speck left anywhere on the ground around them.

Ike watched Milton and Morris. Now, that was taking aim and firing true. "I've got to get Milton to teach me that card trick," said Ike.

Consolidation

Button Row was in an uproar. The back doors to all three houses were propped open. Girl cousins, aunts, and sisters all scurried in and out, carrying armloads of household goods. Mother's skirt hoop sat on the yard table for God and all of Keokuk to see.

"What's going on?" Ike asked Susannah, following her from the back door of his house into the next-door kitchen of hers.

"Consolidation." Susannah deposited a stack of sheets unceremoniously on the table next to the butter dish and turned back to Ike's house.

He hurried to keep up with her. "Why'd

you take our sheets?" he asked, as more things from his house passed in the arms of others. LouLou was holding the corners of her pinafore, making a lumpy sling. She stumbled and an arrowhead fell out.

"Wait!" Ike stopped her. He inspected her jumble: arrowheads, stones, checkers, photo of the Button men. "Those are my things!"

Susannah helped LouLou secure her pinafore and gave her a nudge to send her on her way, but Ike grabbed LouLou's shoulders.

"Give me my things!"

LouLou let go of her pinafore corners, letting everything drop to the ground as she ran crying for Jane.

"Why did LouLou have my collections?" Ike demanded as he knelt to gather everything into a pile.

"We're going to *do* something. Finally," Susannah said.

Ike ignored her as he inspected an arrowhead. "It's got a crack!" he wailed.

"It was already cracked," said Susannah. "Think about it. Twenty-one people in three houses. That makes sense. But twelve? We can fit easily into two houses and put the third to use while the men are gone. You'll go to Aunt Betsy's. She's got a cot in the pantry. Your mother and the girls will stay with Mother and me. That way we have one quiet house for your mother's nerves, and I can be free of those babies and do something useful."

"Free of the babies?"

"You'll be there. They like you."

"Me? No! And what about my house?"

"We could rent the rooms to visiting officers; like a boardinghouse. Or make and sell patriotic trinkets in the parlor. Or dresses. It hasn't actually been decided. I've got a *lot* of ideas."

"But it's *my* house!" Ike ran ahead of her up the stairs to his room. The bed was stripped and his shelf was bare, except for his remaining marbles and Lincoln. Lincoln looked more serious than the Button men. *As Lincoln has called . . .* his father's words came back to him. Surely Lincoln hadn't called him to give up his room.

Ike turned slowly, looking at the four walls of the room he'd slept in every night of his life. Only one of them by himself. His shoes were still by the door. They'd sat to the right of the door every night of his life; Leon's to the left of the door, and Jim's to the left of Leon's.

Jim's shoes had passed to Leon and then to Ike. Ike's old shoes were under the bed, awaiting the potential but unlikely birth of another Button boy. What would Ike do if his feet grew while the men were gone? Ike stuck his bare feet into his shoes. They were a little snug, at that.

He opened his dresser drawer. LouLou hadn't emptied it yet. He pawed through his three shirts, holding each one up to his front successively. He opened Jim's drawer and Leon's. Empty. What if he outgrew his shirts? Could his brothers be gone that long? He flopped on the bare mattress and counted out the forty-seven cracks on the ceiling, a knot of anger growing inside him.

"It's not fair," he said out loud. "They left me here." He sat up. "I'll show them," he said to Lincoln's picture.

He stood at the window. "It's not fair, Barfoot!" he hollered. He grabbed his shirts, clutched the crock of marbles and the picture card, and went to the door.

"What now?" he asked Lincoln, but the president did not reply.

New Room

Ike stood in the middle of his new room. His *temporary* room. Arms outstretched, he touched shelves on both sides, and three long paces took him wall to window. The room was about as big as a soldiering tent. He sat on the floor, setting his collections around him.

Old newspapers were stacked in a corner. *Scrofula, or King's Evil,* read an ad. *One quarter of all our people are scrofulous.* Maybe his mother was always resting because she was scrofulous. Maybe she just needed some Ayers Compound Extract of Sarsaparilla.

He stood up and examined the pantry again. He would only be here until they let him go back to his room, but until then, no

harm in setting it up proper. He unfolded
the legs of the narrow cot and set it against
the wall under the lowest shelf.

"Ike!" LouLou and Jane peered in the
door. "Come draw new paper dolls for us."

"And us!" cried the little girl cousins
crowding in behind them.

"I'm busy," Ike said, and he pulled shut
the door that separated his quarters from
the kitchen.

Rhubarb jelly jars joined sweet gher-
kins on the top shelf, with one pickle jar set
under his cot for snacking. Sugar he scooped
into an empty flour sack by hand and he
dropped bags of beans and boxed this-and-
thats into the newly empty drawer. This left
a whole cleared shelf for his collections, plus
the countertop.

He stacked his extra shirts, pants, nightshirt, and underclothes beneath the cot,
opened the small window, then plumped his
pillow and lay down.

He watched a spider drop from the

ceiling on invisible silk. He missed his forty-seven cracks.

He folded his hands on his chest. The walls were too close.

He twiddled his thumbs. It was all wrong, lying down in a pantry. There wasn't even room next to the door for his shoes. He'd had to put them under the cot.

He closed his eyes and tried to imagine himself in a smart uniform with a bayonet across his chest, in a tent with his brothers. Uncle Palmer must have slept in a tent, too, out west. The babies were crying, a sound he couldn't imagine into any battlefield or gold-panning scene.

He would find a way to go south. He would show them.

"Ike!" Aunt Betsy called, tapping on his door. "Bring a jar of jelly for the babies, will you?"

First Letter

The men had been gone eight days when the first letter arrived.

Ike found his mother nursing her nerves in Aunt Sue's bedroom. Jane and LouLou were playing war with paper dolls on the floor next to the bed.

"Mother," he said loudly from the doorway. "Mail."

"LouLou shot Queen Victoria!" Jane whined as soon as Mother opened her eyes.

Ike held up the letter.

"Give it to me!" Mother exclaimed.

Jane handed her the doll, but Mother waved her off and beckoned Ike into the room.

"You should get out of bed," he mumbled, stepping over the paper dolls. Mother sat up and grabbed the envelope from him, clutching it to her chest.

"Daniel," she whispered. "Go get the others, Ike. We'll open it all together in the parlor. Girls, go downstairs and straighten up."

Aunt Betsy was spooning mush into the mouths of the babies.

"We got a letter," Ike said. "Mother says to come over."

"Glory be!" Aunt Betsy boomed. "Grace Gorman has had two already. Sarah Mallory, too." She opened the door. "Susannah! Gather the girls. On the double!" She handed a baby to Ike and put her hands on her ample hips. "That mother of yours out of bed yet?"

"Yes, Aunt Betsy," he said, thankful that he'd seen his mother sit up before he'd left so he didn't have to lie. He pulled the baby's hand out of his hair and set her on the floor.

"Good. That's the spirit. Now, go get plates and forks and take them to the yard table. Good thing Sue and I have been keeping up with our baking."

"Susannah!" she hollered. "Tell your mother to bring a pie!"

"I'm right here," said Aunt Sue from the porch. "Is Olive out of bed?"

"Yes!" said Ike as he balanced a stack of plates.

"Olive, we'll meet outside!" Aunt Sue called.

"I heard," Ike's mother said, joining them.

Aunt Betsy started to take the envelope from Mother, but she clutched it tight.

"My son delivered it; I'll read," she said firmly. They all followed her out the door. LouLou and Jane stood by with hankies.

"June the 15th," Mother read.

"The fifteenth!" Aunt Sue exclaimed.

"A week!" Betsy cried. "Well. Suppose it had to walk here. Go on, Olive."

"Our dear families," Mother continued.

She stopped and put her hand to her mouth. Jane held out her hankie but Mother waved her off.

"*We together pen this missive from Hannibal, Missouri, on which shores we have safely stepped.*"

"Hannibal, Missouri!" echoed Aunt Betsy. "Well, now. Fancy our soldiers in *Hannibal!*"

"And farther by now," said Susannah.

The girls started chattering.

"Quiet!" said Aunt Sue. "There's more, there's more. Read on, dear."

"Thank you, Sue," said Mother, managing a smile. She held the letter out and stood taller.

"*We have joined up with General Lyon, who leads us on our next—*"

"Lion!" gasped LouLou.

"Quiet!" everyone shouted. LouLou ran to Ike. He pushed her away. *Leon and Jim with a general?*

". . . our next journey, which is by rail."

"Rail!" Ike shouted, and no one shushed him. None of them had yet ridden a train.

". . . which is by rail," his mother repeated, and continued. "Yes, your men will travel deep into Missouri on the railroad. With love and devotion."

She turned the letter over. She shook the envelope.

"General Lyon?" Aunt Sue said, grabbing the letter and reading it for herself. She handed it back to Ike's mother and hurried inside, returning with a newspaper.

"General Lyon landed four miles below Booneville and opened a heavy cannonade against the rebels, who retreated and dispersed into the adjacent woods, from whence, hidden behind bushes and trees, they opened a brisk fire upon our troops.

"General Lyon then ordered a hasty retreat to the boats . . ." She paused, skimming, then continued. ". . . faced his troops about, bringing *the whole force of his artillery to bear, opened a murderous fire on the rebels . . . then moved forward and took possession of Booneville."*

No one spoke.

"What else did our men say?" asked Aunt Betsy. "There must be more to the letter."

"Nothing else!" Mother said. "We don't even know which one wrote it!"

"*Our next journey* . . . Unsatisfactory. Grace Gorman had a *very* newsy note including stories of a Missouri woman shaking her fist and spitting at the soldiers, and another gifting them with cake the moment they stepped off the *Jeannie Deans*. Also, flags of enormous proportion. None of their men said anything about brisk or murderous fire. We don't know it was our men with General Lyon."

"Brisk fire," said Ike. "What if they were shot?"

"Whose handwriting does it look like?"

Aunt Betsy asked, reaching for the letter. But Mother held it closer and studied it.

"I don't know. I don't know! They've never written to us before!" She dropped the letter, burst into tears, and ran inside.

Ike picked up the letter and put it in his pocket.

"Who's for pie?" asked Aunt Betsy. "Time for pie if ever there was one."

She cut two thick slabs and handed both to Ike.

"One for you, and one for your trusty steed."

Writing a Letter

"I'm taking Barfoot out for a ride," Ike said after supper, which they were eating tonight in Aunt Betsy's dining room. He went to the sideboard for another bite of potatoes as Susannah cleared the dishes.

"Not now," said Aunt Betsy. "Now we write letters."

"But I take Barfoot out every night." Ike nabbed a biscuit as Jane took the plate.

"Not now," said Aunt Sue. "Our men need our support."

"Albirdie will be expecting me for checkers." He watched LouLou wrestle with the milk pitcher.

"Not now, Ike!" snapped Aunt Betsy. Ike looked up. Aunt Betsy didn't snap.

"OK," he mumbled.

"OK," Aunt Betsy said. She wiped down the long table and put out a stack of paper. The younger girls took their paper to the floor, where they lay on their stomachs and drew pictures with stubby pencils. The babies slept on the sofa.

Susannah sat at the table next to Ike. "Baking pies, sweeping the carpet, all these ordinary chores. All this *waiting*. What is there to write about?"

Aunt Betsy unfurled a brand-new map and tacked it to the wall.

"We can keep track of the Iowa First on this map. Ike, make a mark on Hannibal." She put her thick thumb on the word.

Ike ran his hand over the map. He traced the Mississippi from Keokuk to Hannibal. It was barely a pinky finger's distance. How hard would it be to go that far? He drew an

X on Hannibal. "Should I add Booneville?" he asked.

"No," said Aunt Betsy firmly. "We'll only record what we know for sure."

Ike looked for Booneville, pressed his finger on it, then went back to his blank paper.

"Do we have to write to all of them?" he asked.

"No," said his mother. "Just write to who you want to write to." She sat up taller in her chair as she said this.

Dear Leon and Jim, Ike wrote. He held his pencil above the paper for a long time. What would his brothers want to hear? They wouldn't want to hear about Mother crying for them or about Jane and LouLou fighting.

"Can we tell about the house?"

"No!" said all the mothers at once.

Ike studied the page for a long time. . . . *hidden behind bushes and trees.* He doodled around the edges. He wanted to say something to impress his brothers, to make them wish they'd brought him along. But all he'd done so far was bring water in for dishes, watch the babies for Aunt Betsy, ride downtown on Barfoot to watch the new soldiers come into town, meet Junior at the river to shoot rocks with slingshots, and lose several dozen checkers games to Albirdie. Three wins.

He set the pencil down and drummed his fingers on the table. He should be in Missouri, too. He should be on that train. He should be wherever they were right now.

"Quit that drumming, Ike!" Susannah said. "You're interrupting my concentration."

Ike looked at his restless fingers. He looked around the room. Three women. Eight girls. He longed for one of Leon's belches or for Jim to sock him on the arm. He tapped out a quick rhythm on the table with his index fingers.

I have taken up drumming for real, Ike wrote. It was sort of true — he'd tried to get a drumstick from Milton and Morris. It was true in the way that the great traverse from the east was true. Their horses had been stolen, but Palmer had had the fortitude to continue anyhow.

If Palmer didn't need his own horse to set off for the west, why would Ike need a steamer to go south?

He used his pencil to drum another rhythm. There must be a way. Other boats. Ike stood suddenly. He ran to the door and looked across the alley at the Hinman house.

In fact, there were other boats. In fact, a river captain lived very close by with two clever sons. Sons who knew how to get what they wanted.

Maybe soon I will join you. Your brother, Ike.

"There," he said, folding his paper. Everyone else was still writing. His mother let out a loud sniffle now and again. Susannah finished writing and stormed back to her house.

He paused. Reading over his letter again, he saw he sounded like a child, not a soldier. He crouched down and surreptitiously stuck it under the rug with the straw padding. He'd try again when he had something better to say.

"I'm going out," he said quietly, and no one looked up as he made his way out the door, past Barfoot, who snorted noisily, and into the unfamiliar territory of the Hinmans' yard.

Friend or Foe

Ike stood at the Hinmans' back door for a long moment, Goldenrod and Marigold at his side, yapping. *Why would a Hinman help a Button,* he wondered. Well, he'd just have to make Milton and Morris want to go south, too. He took a deep breath and knocked.

"Myrtle!" Old Man Hinman called to his daughter. "Door!"

"Morris!" Mrs. Hinman called. "Door!"

"Milton!" Morris called from upstairs. "You're supposed to get the door."

Ike knocked again.

"Banker, robber, friend, or foe?" called Mrs. Hinman in a singsong voice.

"Ike Button," Ike shouted.

"Oh, a *Button* knocks on our door," called Mrs. Hinman. "Well, now, these must be wartimes indeed. Come in, *Mister* Button."

The Hinman house was laid out much like Ike's and the other Button houses. But the families hadn't spoken since Ike could remember. Some mess with money. He hadn't been in their house since he was young. Milton and Morris had knocked him off the lean-to roof when he was seven and he'd given them a wide berth since.

Ike followed Mrs. Hinman's voice through the kitchen to the front room. Old Mr. Hinman was holding his arms straight out with yarn stretched between them, which Mrs. Hinman was rolling into a ball.

"Isaac Button. In my very front room. I guess now that the men are gone, no telling what all is going to change.

"And speaking of change, I saw out our upstairs window *much* ado at Button Row some days back. *Much* carrying on of personal items from one door to the next. What on earth?"

"Con-con-consolidation," Ike stammered. "Twenty-one people, three houses . . . eleven . . . It's just that . . . What are you doing with all that yarn?" Why didn't Milton and Morris come downstairs and rescue him?

"Blame rubbish, ask me," Old Man Hinman snapped with a furious glance at his daughter that she didn't see.

"There is no call for such a tone, Daddy," Mrs. Hinman said. "Isaac had no choice about being born a Button, now, did you?"

"I meant this darned string," the old man muttered.

Mrs. Hinman ignored him and kept winding the yarn at a dizzying speed.

"Socks," she said. "Our boys are going to need socks. Even the Button boys. This scuffle is going to last longer than a pair of stockings per man, you take it from Myrtle

Hinman, river captain's wife. River captains, unlike mere lounge-abouts, need respectable socks on a regular basis." She came to the end of the skein and plopped the ball into a waiting basket with a satisfied *humph.*

"Are the Button women doing their knitting?" she asked, holding up a stocking, then picking away at the stitches. "And you? Boys can knit, too, you know. My Morris and Milton are doing their part, I don't mind telling you. They're upstairs stitching woollies right now. Not only for their own people, but also for whoever may be in need. Are you knitting?"

"I, um, I . . ."

"Tsk-tsk," said Mrs. Hinman. "Rolling bandages? Picking lint?"

Ike shook his head.

"Just as I thought. Though, it isn't really your fault no one has instilled these values in you. We have to *pull* together, Isaac. Despite that anti-slave nonsense, we are a nation. And a nation is like a family. And family sticks together. Our nation must *pull* together. Isn't that right, Daddy?"

Old Man Hinman picked up a newspaper and held it in front of his face. He grunted noncommittally.

"Daddy would have gone to war, too, even at his advanced age, if it weren't for his afflicted lungs."

Old Man Hinman mustered a hearty cough.

"As it is, my sister's family sent eight boys all told. I don't mind telling you that their regimental leader says they're gifted at the drums and fife. Rhythm. They got that from my people. They are an asset to the Union, and they shall have dry feet."

Mrs. Hinman set down her needles. "But I can't do it all myself, Isaac. I was just saying to Daddy, I says, *What this neighborhood needs is a Soldiers' Aid Society.* Didn't I say just that, Daddy? I'd host it here, heaven knows, but look around you, Isaac. There isn't a whit of room in here, what with Daddy's books and newspapers and what have you. A *globe,* for the love of Pete. Now, if we had resources from out west, like *some people,* resources that are quite due us, this might well be Hinman Row instead of just the Hinman house, and we'd have plenty of room to share with the community."

She picked up her needles and knit with a fury.

"But that's water under the bridge, isn't it? Captain Hinman said to me last time he was home, he says, *Water under the bridge, dearest. Let it be water under the bridge.* And I must let it be. What we need is a generous space that could be used at any hour. A place for neighbor women to gather. To store our supplies. To come *together* in community to *aid* our men in battle."

"I just came to see . . ." Ike started. How could he ask her to let him see Milton and Morris?

Mrs. Hinman's hands stopped. She looked up from her knitting. Then she threw down her needles and stood up.

"Why, you dear boy! Of course! And here I've been babbling when all the while you'd come here with an olive branch. A dove *and* a solution. Did you hear that, Daddy? Oh, the Lord works in mysterious ways. From the mouth of a Button. Well, I'll be."

She took Ike's shoulders and squeezed him into a hug.

Ike pulled away in alarm and looked at Old Man Hinman, who shrugged.

"I must tell all the ladies," Mrs. Hinman said, pacing the room. "We'll need food, of course, and an organizational leader. That will be me. Though, if your mother would like to cochair, having offered her home and all, well, that could be arranged. Tell your mother and aunties that we'll start next week Tuesday. That will give them a couple of days to get the house in shape. We must operate a tidy ship."

"My house?" Ike said, grasping now what Mrs. Hinman was assuming. "But . . ."

"No, never fear. My pride is not hurt, dear boy. You can tell your mother that. It's time to set aside our differences, what with the men gone. My Horace will be back, of course, on the next packet or the one after that, if he isn't detained for some business or other. Now, I've got plenty to do to get ready. Thank you for your visit."

Mrs. Hinman waved for Ike to leave. He hesitated, then eased his way around her to the base of the steps.

"I'll just ask Milton and Morris to teach me to . . . um . . . knit," he said, and pounded up the steps before she could object.

Milton and Morris

Ike found Morris and Milton in the room identical to his real room. Except that they had their own beds. They were on the floor, with playing cards spread out everywhere. Two balls of red yarn sat in a corner, impaled with knitting needles.

"Button," said Milton, jumping to his feet. He stood directly in front of Ike, blocking his view of the room. "Where's Albirdie?"

"Home. I don't know. Not here."

"We were just sorting."

"*Fixing,*" said Morris. "We're fixing the decks for a new trick. I don't care if he knows."

Milton went back to his cards, and Ike looked around the room. The boys had more decks of cards than he'd ever seen in one place. Also, heaps of marbles. And twine and a length of copper, leather squares, matches, a soldier's canteen, a pile of drumsticks. A treasure trove. How had he not been here before? Wouldn't Albirdie love to see this!

"Where did it all come from?" he asked.

"We are observers," said Milton.

"Hunters," Morris put in, still sorting. "Not bad, huh? So, why are you here?"

Ike drew himself up. He felt like Palmer, fording the Missouri, making his way. He reached for that knot of anger and injustice that had been festering since Leon and Jim had left him standing on the shore while the *Jeannie Deans* steamed away.

"Let's go south," he said.

They set down their cards and looked at Ike.

"For what? The Iowa First is already gone," said Milton.

"Why should we be left here with the women? The men have started fighting. We could go, too."

"We?" they said at once.

"Well, with your father being a river captain, you could get us downriver, right? Couldn't we get passage on his packet? Or stow away? We only need to get as far as Hannibal, then get the train to wherever the war is."

Ike took a breath. They were still paying attention, so he continued. "We bring drumsticks, see. And if anyone asks, we're with the drum corps. Some of the boys didn't have uniforms yet, so that won't be a problem. And once we get there, well, some regiment will take us."

"Huh," said Milton. He looked at Morris.

"Albirdie won that compass off just one soldier," Ike said. "Imagine what you could scavenge with all those soldiers together."

The boys leaned forward.

"You don't want to stay here with the women, do you?" Ike asked, picking up the yarn and needles. "Your mother's going to make you use these."

"But Pa would never let us—" said Morris.

"Quiet," Milton interrupted. "A boat, huh?"

"That's why I thought of you. I have weapons and other provisions. I could have done this all on my own, found a small raft, but I thought, since I had such a good plan, well, I'd let you in on it. And you're so good at . . . problem solving that I thought you'd want to find us the transportation."

Milton and Morris looked at each other.

"That sounds like a lot of work," said Morris. "We have a lot going on here."

Ike looked around the room. It was true. "You're good at cards. You must be running out of chumps here."

"He makes a point," said Milton.

"We want Albirdie's compass," announced Morris. "Get Albirdie's compass and we'll find a boat."

"I can't," said Ike. He walked to the window and looked across the yards to his house. "I can get us a map."

"I'm with Milton on this one, Ike," Morris said. "The compass. Leave the boat to us."

"And don't tell anyone. We can't let any word reach our ma. She finds out she'll have our hides," said Milton.

"Not even Albirdie," said Morris.

"Especially not Albirdie Woolley," said Milton. "I don't trust a girl who can beat Morris at checkers. Besides, her daddy being a preacher, she'd blab the whole thing."

"Preachers have a way of dragging a story out of a fellow," Morris agreed, shaking his head. "Remember, Milt, when you . . ."

"Never mind that," said Milton, whapping his brother. "Just keep it quiet, Ike.

Work on getting that compass, and wait for me to figure it out."

"What if Ike can't keep quiet?" Morris asked. "I bet he tells his girlfriend everything."

"She's not my girlfriend!"

"Whatever you say, Ike." Morris and Milton made smooching sounds.

"Albirdie's a priss," Ike offered, feeling bold and weak at the same time.

Milton and Morris laughed.

"Scram, Ike. We'll find you when we're ready."

Ike trudged across the Hinman yard and passed Barfoot without looking at him. This should feel exciting. He had made a plan. He was going to do something. Like Uncle Palmer, he had fortitude. Albirdie would understand.

Designing Destiny

Ike was shelling peas on the back step, keeping an eye out for Milton and Morris and considering how to get the compass from Albirdie, when he overheard Susannah say to her mother, "Kate from Kentucky is taking nurse's training. She told me yesterday. She said I should, too."

Ike stood up fast, upsetting the basket.

Kate.

Leon's note. The peas rolled down the steps and into the dirt. Barfoot raised his head and trotted over. Ike reached into his pockets. Two pebbles, a checkers piece. No note. He shooed Barfoot away from the peas and ran into his small room. His other pair of pants was stuffed under the cot. There. In his pocket. Wrinkled but intact.

"The Keokuk Buttons have offered six sons to Lincoln, and three fathers. I am not adding you to the tally," Aunt Sue was saying when Ike came out. He scooped peas back into the basket.

"Thomas says the Union's going to prevail before his regiment even gets to go," said Susannah. "*Prevail,* Mama. He's educated. Besides, Kate says they need us here in Keokuk."

"If the war's over before they get called up, they won't need you at the hospital. There are enough nurses already to take care of carousing soldiers and cranky old men. Now, go get the peas from Ike."

Susannah stomped out the door, letting it slam behind her. "Peas," she demanded.

Ike handed her what he had gathered, including quite a few pods and some dirt.

"Do you know where Kate is?" he said. "I have this for her."

"Kate, Kate, Kate. That's all anyone ever talks about around here," Susannah said. "I suppose you're in love with her, too."

"No!" said Ike. "It's Leon." He held out the note.

Susannah grabbed it from him. She took the peas inside and came back out. "Have you read it?" she asked.

"No," said Ike. "I forgot about it. And it's sealed."

Susannah pried the sealing wax loose with her fingernail. She unfolded the note, skimmed it, and refolded it, pressing the wax back in place.

"Let me see," said Ike.

"It's private," said Susannah.

"But . . ."

"But we will bring it to her," said Susannah. "Come on." She rushed out of the yard, and Ike hurried to keep up with her.

"I can't."

"Yes, you can."

"But I'm expecting . . ." He stopped.

"What?" Susannah stopped in the middle of the street and turned to look at him. "What are you expecting?"

"Nobody. Nothing."

"Good." She resumed at a clip.

"Where are we going?" Ike asked as they passed Kate's house and turned up Eighth Street, toward downtown.

"Ellis Hotel. That's where they do the training. Kate says it's going to be turned into a hospital."

"Slow down," said Ike. "It's hot."

"I can't slow down," said Susannah. "I'm too mad. Boys. My brothers. Leon and Jim. Even Thomas. All the boys get to go to war."

"Not me," Ike interjected.

"Doesn't count," said Susannah.

"But—"

"You *could* go if you were older. If it goes on long enough, you *can* go. That's the point.

Me? What can I do? Watch Aunt Betsy's girls. Watch your sisters. Bake pies. Scour the floor with river sand."

"And pull lint for bandages with the ladies," Ike offered.

Susannah grabbed Ike by the arm and spun him toward her.

"Exactly. Exactly! At least you see what I mean." She let him go and started off again at her long-legged pace. Ike scrambled to catch up.

"Oh, to dream of pulling lint for bandages," she said dramatically, throwing her arms out wide, "when the boys are out saving the union of these United States."

"They're really just riding a train so far," said Ike.

"No," said Susannah. "They are designing the destiny of our nation while we sit here, you and me, shelling peas and wiping noses and, and, and. Well, not me. Not me, Isaac Nathaniel Button. Not me."

"Me neither!" said Ike. "What are you going to do?" he asked. "Because I want to—"

"Kate," Susannah declared as if that explained everything. She held up the note triumphantly and turned left at Blondeau.

Dashing Kate

A regiment of new soldiers spilled out of the Sterns Building. Susannah and Ike watched the men form themselves into a semblance of orderly lines. A drunk staggered out of Lewis Eck's saloon and pushed his way through the ranks.

"At least there's this," Susannah declared as she pulled Ike out of the road to avoid a galloping horse. "Life. Activity. Soldiers."

They slowed as they got to Main. Susannah smoothed her hair with her hand while they waited to cross and turned to Ike. "How do I look?" she demanded.

Ike studied her. She just looked like his cousin. Tall. Stern. Bony elbows that had found him all too often. He couldn't think what words he was supposed to say.

"Humph," she said. "A simple compliment to boost my confidence would have done fine, Ike." She started across the street.

"Confidence for what?"

But then they were across and standing in front of the Ellis Hotel. "Wait here," Susannah said.

Ike watched her disappear into a sea of white coats and white dresses. A man with one leg came up behind him and whacked Ike with his crutch. "Give a veteran some respect here, son."

Ike jumped aside and opened the door for him, watching him hobble inside. There were several veterans in town missing arms or legs from previous wars. Ike touched his own leg. What if Leon or Jim had lost a limb? He wandered down the street, stopping to read a poster nailed to the wall of Cutts & Simms Umbrella Sales and Repair.

HORSE STOLEN
$50 Reward! ~

$50 REWARD WILL BE PAID
FOR DELIVERY TO ME, OF MY STALLION,
WHICH WAS STOLEN FROM THE STABLE,
ON THE NIGHT OF JUNE 2D, 1861.

This Horse is a Fine Jet Black,
about 15 hands high, with
ONE HIND FOOT WHITE.
He is a MORGAN HORSE
of fine carriage, and a
FAST SQUARE TROTTER.
He has a Scar on One of His Hind
Pastern Joints, caused by getting his foot
over the halter, which has just healed up.

Thos. W. Clagett, Keokuk, Iowa.

Fifty dollars! But more than the money, a horse. Fine jet-black. Fifteen hands high. Where a fellow could go on a Morgan of fine carriage. Barfoot had been old always, it seemed, and truth be told, Ike longed to feel speed. He looked into the street as if the horse would just appear. He turned back to study the notice again, and his eyes roamed to the next poster over.

Runaway from the subscriber, Clark County, Mo. Negro woman named MARY, and two boys.

He turned away. These posters made his stomach tighten. What made one colored person a slave or criminal and another free? There were colored people in Keokuk. If they went across the river into Missouri, would they be enslaved? And if Iowa was a Free State, why were they on wanted posters? It was easier not to think about it. He forced himself to read the horse poster again, but his eyes wandered back.

RUN AWAY
FROM THE SUBSCRIBER

CLARK COUNTY, MO.
NEGRO WOMAN NAMED
MARY, AND TWO BOYS.

Woman about 36 years old,
tall and of slight build, very black,
very long feet and hands;
had on when she left a
blue calico dress and a sunbonnet;
no other clothing.

Boys DAVID, 11, JOHN, 7.

Will pay a liberal REWARD.

Runaway. Run away. Wasn't that what he wanted to do? And was it wrong to run away when there was a reason, like going south to join the army? To design destiny?

A hand came from behind Ike's back and tore the poster smartly off the wall. It was Albirdie's father, with Albirdie coming up behind him. He rolled the poster up quickly and tucked it inside his vest.

"Let that be a lesson to you, Isaac," said Reverend Woolley.

"Which lesson?" asked Ike, avoiding Albirdie's eyes. The less chance he had of spilling his plan with Milton and Morris the better.

They were interrupted by the looming presence of Mr. Cutts and Mr. Simms, who'd stumbled out of Ohmer's Saloon across the street. They stunk like liquor and sweat and had guns hanging from belts around their ample waists.

"Blame fools," Reverend Woolley said under his breath. "Sunny-day nuisances." He took a step back. Ike and Albirdie stepped back, too.

"Gentlemen," Reverend Woolley said coolly.

"Padre," snarled Cutts, the taller of the two. "I believe you got something what belongs to us."

"That's right," said Simms. "It's illegal to harbor contraband."

"It's a poster, not a person, *sir*," said Reverend Woolley coldly. "And this here's a public wall."

"Aid," amended Cutts. "It's illegal to *aid* a fugitive. Fine of one thousand dollars or six months in jail."

"We won't hurt her," said Simms, sounding suddenly reasonable. "Have you found her?"

"She's got to go back to her rightful owner. Her and all of them sort. It's the law," said Cutts.

The Reverend patted his shirt. "And you're her rightful owner? Here in Keokuk, Iowa? Land of the free?"

"Not us, per se," said Simms. "But we got friends who are bounty hunters. They are hired by that gentleman what's named on the document you have stolen."

"Ah," said the Reverend. "So it's about the money, is it?"

"No," said Cutts. "It's about justice."

"And justice is done. Good day, gentlemen," the Reverend said as if they'd simply said, *Fine weather for a walk*. He stepped smartly around them and off the sidewalk onto the street.

"What are you staring at, kid?" Cutts growled at Ike, and huffed off after the Reverend.

"Come over later?" Albirdie asked Ike.

Ike looked away. He concentrated on his plan with Milton and Morris. "Maybe. Probably not." Where was Susannah?

"Oh," said Albirdie flatly. They stood

awkwardly for a moment, then Albirdie followed her father. Mr. Jenkins stood in the doorway of the barbershop. He inclined his head to Reverend Woolley and Albirdie, then stepped inside. Cutts and Simms walked a few paces behind.

Ike glanced at the empty spot on the wall. He remembered seeing Mr. Jenkins at the church the night the *Jeannie Deans* arrived, and what Milton and Morris had said about the men at the junkyard. Could Albirdie's father be arrested? Albirdie, too?

"Ike!" It was Susannah at last.

"Now what?" he said, running toward her. "When do we find Kate? I need to get home."

"We did!" Susannah said. She held up a book triumphantly. *NOTES ON NURSING: What It Is and What It Is Not.* "I did. And now there's this. I'm going to study at home and take the test when Kate does. She's going to help me. And once I've passed, what is Mother going to say?"

"But what did Kate *say*?"

"About what?"

"Leon's note!"

"Oh, that. I gave it to her, then we talked about this." Susannah opened it and started reading while they walked.

"*Disease is a reparative process.* Well, that's something, but I need more. Rules. Tools."

"But did she say something back? Does she have a note for Leon in return? I should send him her reply."

"Leon," Susannah scoffed. "Kate does not have time for the likes of Leon Button. We have things to do, Kate and I."

"What will I tell Leon?" Ike asked.

"Tell him Kate is considering his correspondence with veracity. He won't know what you mean, but he won't want to let you know that."

"But what will I mean?" said Ike.

"It doesn't matter, don't you see?" said Susannah. "Now, walk in front of me and tell me if I'm going to run into anything. I've got reading to do." And she walked directly behind Ike the rest of the way, reading, and quoting out loud anything she thought he would want to know.

Riders

Ike woke to the sound of girls' voices chattering and pans clanking. He opened his eyes and looked directly into a new sack of flour.

Like the last eleven mornings, it all came back to him gradually. This cot. This pantry bedroom. His father, brothers, boy cousins, and uncles in Missouri, all sleeping in tents, their belongings in packs, or lying in the brush, bleeding. His belongings were stacked in the shallow space beneath him, and the hardest thing facing him was avoiding Albirdie. He'd prod Milton and Morris today.

"Good morning, sleepyhead!" Aunt Betsy thundered when he stepped into the kitchen.

"We've et, but bless your tired little heart, you slept right on through. We saved you plenty. Plenty!" He ducked out of her embrace, but she grabbed him and gave him another squeeze. "Grace Gorman sends word that all Keokuk men are intact. Happy day."

The babies squealed from their chairs, where they were secured with dish towels. They held out their arms to Ike.

"Come play with us!" the girls called from the parlor.

Leon and Jim were fine. And they were not picking up babies or entertaining princesses or being squeezed by aunties. Neither were Milton and Morris.

"Not now. I've got to take care of Barfoot," Ike told the babies. "Horsey." He whinnied and they giggled and clapped.

Barfoot had wandered across the alley and was nibbling on the tops of the early carrots coming up in the Hinmans' vegetable patch.

"I'm trying to cultivate produce to feed

my family, young man," Mrs. Hinman called out the window. "Has your mother prepared the house for our meeting?"

"Yes, ma'am. Sorry, ma'am." Ike pulled Barfoot away. "Are Milton and Morris home?"

"No, they are not. My sons have important business to attend to today. They've not got time to loaf about like some boys do."

"What business?" Ike asked, but she had already turned away from the window.

"Come on home, old boy," he said to Barfoot. "You're a nuisance, know that?" What he wouldn't give for a horse like the one on the poster. Probably the cavalry had horses like that. If the war lasted long enough, he would join the cavalry. For now, the infantry would do. There'd be no retreating, then.

Jane and LouLou hollered at Ike out the open window. "Mother says—" But Ike cut them off.

"I'll be back!" he said. "Come on, Barfoot." Milton and Morris could be at the river looking for a boat right now.

Barfoot set out at his own stubborn pace toward the river as Ike leaned forward, urging him on.

Four men passed on tall black horses, riding fast. Hooves pounded like a full drum corps in parade. Their flanks shone as their galloping muscles rippled.

"Hurry, Barfoot," he said, digging his heels into Barfoot's side. "Gallop like they're galloping. Giddyup!"

But Barfoot plodded along, slow as ever.

"Fine, then," Ike muttered.

He slipped off Barfoot's back and ran ahead, cutting over to High Street to avoid the church and the chance of seeing Albirdie. He ran until his lungs hurt and his sweaty shirt clung to his chest, ran as if he were chasing rebel soldiers. He flopped down on the grass under an oak on Water Street. He looked up and saw Barfoot actually trotting toward him. A slow trot, but a trot all the same.

"Barfoot," Ike exclaimed, and ran to him. "Old boy! See? That's the way!"

He led Barfoot to the water and let him drink. Then they walked along the rocky shore. The Mississippi here was like an elbow, with Keokuk tucked inside it. No sign of Milton and Morris.

Ike gazed across the river. "That's Illinois," he told Barfoot. "And over there, Missouri. That's where the rest of the Button men are."

They ambled a bit farther and stopped where the bank went up steep, thick with trees and underbrush. Ike sat on the ground and they watched the sky for eagles.

"Hawk," he said. "Pheasant." A small boat passed with three boys aboard. Not Milton and Morris. They waved as the current carried them slowly downriver.

"They've got a boat," Ike said as Barfoot wandered into the shady protection of the trees.

A pair of stout men on tall stallions mean-dered down the shore. They had guns across their saddles and were looking around as if something or someone would jump out of the bushes at any moment. Ike walked over to admire their horses as they passed.

"Get out of our way, rascal," the first man snarled. Ike watched them go, pretend-ing they were enemy soldiers and he was with the Iowa First.

He loaded his slingshot, took aim at the hat of the rider closest to the water, and fired. The stone arched, then dropped too soon, striking the ground alongside one of the horses. It reared and Ike ducked behind a tree.

"Washington, Adams, Jefferson, Madison, Monroe," he recited. When he got to *Polk* he peered out. All clear. The men had con-trolled the horse and continued on without looking back. Ike stepped into the open and took a few paces toward the river.

If this were real war, those men would have chased him. If this were real war, he could put all his skills to use: tree climbing, finding his way after being lost, carrying heavy objects.

But the real war was far from here. If he didn't get south soon, it would be over before he got to take part.

Ike stuck his slingshot in his back waistband and looked for Barfoot. He paused to pick a handful of berries, stepping into the trees and brambles. "Barfoot!"

Ike whistled, then stopped to listen. There was a rustling farther on. He hopped up on a boulder and jumped to a rotting log, moving stealthily, careful not to make a noise. If this were the South, he'd be tracking the rebs through brush and trees. A twig snapped just ahead.

"Hello?" he called. "Who's there? Milton! Morris!" Nothing. "Guys?" Maybe they were going to leap out at him.

Ike grasped his slingshot and took in his surroundings. Trees, logs, a discarded barrel. They were going to surround him and take him prisoner. He leaped to another log, then dove to the ground and crouched behind the barrel. Still nothing.

He dug a stone out of the ground with his thumb. Too heavy for his slingshot. He was a cannon and this was his cannonball. "Ike Button attacks Colonel Oak!" He tucked the stone under his chin, then launched it, aiming for a low knot in the trunk, but it went left.

"Ow!"

Ike spotted blue calico behind a bush. He crept closer and pulled a branch aside.

It was a woman.

A colored woman.

Crouching on the ground with a tattered bonnet in her hand, rubbing her forehead.

Ike froze.

Slowly, she put the bonnet on her head, then stood, looking down at him.

Like his mother, she wasn't young or old. Her narrow feet were wrapped in strips of cloth instead of shoes, and the hem of her dress was torn and dirty. A wisp of recognition and alarm nudged at the edge of his mind.

There was an angry welt on her forehead, where the stone had struck her.

"I'm sorry," he said.

She shook her head, putting a finger to her lips and looking past him.

Ike glanced behind him. He was alone. Alone in the woods with a colored woman. He wished for Milton and Morris to spring out at him, or even for the men on horses to come back. He wanted to turn and run, but his legs wouldn't obey.

She pulled a small satchel from behind the tree and backed up, waving him away.

Then Ike remembered. The poster.

Runaway from the subscriber . . .

"Mary?" Ike said softly. It felt wrong to address a grown woman by her first name, but the bold letters on the poster had offered no surname. He looked at his feet.

She gasped.

Illegal to harbor contraband. Cutts and Simms's words came back to Ike. *We got friends . . .* Could the riders be Cutts and Simms's bounty hunter friends?

"Please, son," she said slowly.

Her voice was thin like his mother's, and weary.

"Yours is a kind face. If there is a kind heart behind it, walk away and forget what you saw here."

Ike couldn't look at her. His stomach felt sick. He wished he had not come here. But if this were the Mary from the poster, she would have two boys with her. Maybe it wasn't her.

"Do you have two boys?" he asked.

She straightened abruptly and fixed her gaze on him, stepping toward him, twigs snapping under her feet like the pops of a distant gun.

She reached out and touched his arm.

Ike flinched.

"You hurt yourself," she said. He looked down and saw a trickle of blood on his arm. The brambles. She took off her bonnet. There was a wide cloth strap. She pressed one end of it on his arm, dabbing off the blood.

The weight of her hand was rough and warm. "There," she said softly. She looked into his eyes. Her face was startlingly smooth, like a girl's, but her eyes were old and tired. "I do have two boys. We got separated. They'll find a way here. I'm sure of it. My boys are like you. Quick, bad aim. They can't keep a secret for sweets or silver. I don't expect you will, either. But if you could just give me time. Silence. A day. Two. Time for my boys to catch up. And if you have to tell, tell a friend."

Was silence *aid*? He looked up at the woman, then over his shoulder for Barfoot.

Was he supposed to call for help? Ask her to come with him? Turn her in to the sheriff before the bounty hunters found out she was here?

"I'm sorry," he mumbled. He spun around and ran. He stumbled over tree roots and snagged his pants on a bramble. He looked back and saw Mary watching. Then she turned and disappeared into the thick.

Skedaddle

"Barfoot!" Ike pulled Barfoot's snout out of the daisy patch at the boardinghouse on Water Street. He leaned his forehead into his horse's neck and took a deep breath, then another. He wished he could unsee what he'd seen. A carriage clattered by and Ike ducked under Barfoot's belly and stood out of sight of the street.

"You there!"

Ike jumped. Mrs. Kraft burst out of the boardinghouse door and waved a rolling pin at him. Did she know? Was she going to turn him in?

"Your nag is blocking my view of the street, young man. Skedaddle!"

A bee buzzed up out of the flowers just then and landed on Barfoot's nose. Barfoot snorted in alarm, shook his head back and forth, then took off at a near trot. Ike ran after him, shouting over his shoulder, "He's a he!"

Barfoot slowed back to his usual walk after a block and a half and stopped to drink out of the birdbath at the McGoverns'.

"We need to find Milton and Morris, Barfoot. Come on, boy, come on."

They trudged up Morgan and into the alley, then circled the Hinman house. "Milton! Morris!" Ike hollered up at their window, but there was no response. Goldenrod and Marigold were inside barking, and the yard was empty.

The windows at Ike's own house were open and there was a jumble of women's voices, and Albirdie was walking briskly down the alley and into his yard.

She didn't look like herself. She had on a clean calico dress and her hair was neatly pulled back. The story of Mary nearly fell right out of his mouth, but she jumped in first.

"Aren't you coming?" She turned and marched toward the porch, and despite his resolve to maintain his distance from Albirdie, Ike found himself following her.

"Where? Why are you dressed up? Did something happen to the men?"

But before she could answer, they'd reached his house, the house he'd been consolidated out of, from which came a great racket of voices, and Albirdie Woolley walked right in as if she'd been invited.

The front room was full of women. Dining chairs were interspersed with parlor chairs, and Mrs. Hinman stood in the center of it all, Ike's mother at her side, her eyes weary, but wearing her company smile. *Mary.*

Milton and Morris were in the dining room, serving themselves wide wedges of pie. Ike backed toward the door.

". . . each responsible for . . ." Mrs. Hinman was saying, but Ike interrupted.

"Is there news?"

"No, young man, there is no news, and *you*"—she pointed her finger at Albirdie—"Albirdie Woolley. Why, I never."

"You called for the women of the neighborhood, so my father sent me, since we have no other woman in our household." She stepped over the little girls and wedged herself a spot on the sofa between Susannah and Mrs. Gorman. "Come on, Ike." She pointed to the footstool in front of Mrs. Gorman, who moved her feet obligingly.

"Well. I . . . *All right*," said Mrs. Hinman with an air of resignation. "But, Miss Woolley, keep in mind that we are a Soldiers' Aid Society, gathered in an effort to help our men at war. We are not going to get mixed up in any of that abolitionist talk of your father's. I dare say, we are women of varied notions that may otherwise separate us, but the notion that brings us together here is *service*." She looked around the room, slowly, taking in each face as she spoke solemnly. "We are not here to discuss politics."

"OK, OK, now, Myrtle," said Aunt Betsy. "Let's get back to business, shall we?"

"Ike!" Morris said loudly.

"Hush, now, pet, and eat your pie," said Mrs. Hinman.

Albirdie grabbed Ike's arm as he stood to go, but he brushed her away and picked his way over shoes and skirt hems to the dining room.

"Just the man we're looking for," said Milton. "Let's get out of here."

Ike looked at Albirdie. She shook her head furiously.

"Come on," Morris said. Milton held out a deck of cards.

Ike avoided Albirdie's angry stare and followed the boys out to the yard table.

"Has your dad come back?" Ike asked in a low voice. "When will we leave?"

"Do you have the compass?"

"No."

"There you go, then," said Milton. "We'll take care of the boat once you have the compass."

"But I said a map."

"Do you have a map?"

"My aunt Betsy has a map on the wall in her house. I'll get that."

"A wall map?" said Morris. "That's too big. What you don't know about boat travel is that everything needs to be compact. What we need is a map about this big." He held out his hands in a small rectangle.

"I can make one," said Ike. "I'll do it now."

"Just make it right," said Morris.

"We'll leave tomorrow," Ike said. "Agreed?"

"Tomorrow, the next day . . ."

"Tomorrow," said Ike, and then repeated it. "Tomorrow."

Ricochet

"Ike!" Jane hollered. "Mother says Barfoot needs food!"

"Barfoot needs food!" LouLou echoed. Jane was teaching LouLou and the little cousins to skip. An army of hard-soled shoes ricocheted like bullets off the porch boards, while Ike sat on the floor in his old room, pencil poised over the Mississippi. The floor was heaped with linens donated for the war effort. A bolt of yellow calico, a jumble of pillow slips, a stack of thread-bare but freshly washed sheets, waiting to be made into handkerchiefs.

"And water!" Jane called.

"And water!" LouLou echoed.

"I know!" he hollered back. He had Aunt Betsy's map spread out and was copying it — with great attention to detail and scale — onto a small sheet of paper. It was hard to concentrate, and if he could think of any other way to get a boat, he would leave Milton and Morris out of the whole plan.

Drawing the river coming north made Ike think about Mary, and he set down his pencil. The longest he'd ever kept a secret was . . . never. And something like this? It filled his stomach with dread. He hadn't been able to manage a whole boiled egg for breakfast, much less a biscuit. Usually, the ritual of puzzling out his men on a checkerboard with Albirdie settled his insides. But that was before. He went to the window, hoping to see Milton and Morris coming to get him.

Ike studied what he'd drawn. It didn't look as though it could keep them from getting lost, but it would have to do. This is how Palmer must have felt as he set out for the west: like there was no steady ground under his feet, yet a whole new world was before him. No more home problems; no more waiting.

He had one thing left to do. Mary had said if he did tell, to make sure it was a friend. If he passed it on to someone else, would his secret stop gnawing at him? That was it. Susannah. Susannah was more than a friend. She was family.

He ventured past the skipping girls into Aunt Sue's empty kitchen.

"Susannah!" he called. There was no answer.

LouLou and Jane and the little girls clamored in.

"Did you feed Barfoot?" they said. "Let us ride him!"

"Later." Ike grabbed the pail from the porch, dodged skipping Jane, and pumped water from the well. He carried the bucket to the lean-to. There was Susannah,

136

nestled between two straw bales, a mug of water in her hand and a book open on her lap.

"Shhh!" she hissed.

"What are you—?"

"Shhh!" she said again.

Ike sat down beside her.

"What are you doing here?" he whispered. She held up her nursing book. "Avoiding them," she said. "Listen to this. *A dark house is always an unhealthy house, always an ill-aired house. . . . Want of light stops growth and promotes scrofula, rickets, etc., among the children.*"

"Susannah, I've got to tell you something."

"Not now. Quiz me," she said. "I've got nearly this whole section memorized. She held the book out to Ike. "Just sit down! Don't let my mother see that you're talking to someone."

Ike sat on the ground, out of sight of the house.

"Kate heard from Mrs. Hinman that they'll be taking women as nurses in the field, and I promised not to tell, because her mother and my mother would have fits, but if I learn this, we can join up."

Ike studied his cousin warily. He had to tell someone or he'd explode. Someone he could trust. And maybe Albirdie would lend him the compass.

"I'll be back," said Ike. "I've got somewhere to be."

"Wait!" said Susannah. "Ike!"

"If Milton and Morris come over, tell them I'll be right back."

Rematch

Ike found Albirdie lying on her stomach on the back pew with a long sheet of paper flattened in front of her, pencil poised above it.

"Albirdie," he said. She held up one finger. He stood and waited, peering over her shoulder. She made a mark on the page, then used a straightedge to make another.

"Albirdie," he said again. Lines and angles and squares and a tiny person. The compass anchored one corner of the page.

She shook her head and held up her finger again. Then slapped her pencil down and sat up.

"There," she said proudly. "I'm so good at this."

Ike slid into the pew, picked up the compass, and turned the page to face him. He felt the weight of the compass in his hand. It was still on the string Albirdie used to hang it around her neck.

"It's a map," she said.

"I know. But of what?"

She made a small umbrella along one line, and some small circles across from it.

"Keokuk," she said, reaching for the compass. Ike pulled it back.

"I'm just looking at it." He set the compass on the edge of the map. "Why Keokuk?"

"It's where we live. Here's Cutts & Simms Umbrella, ice cream at Ohmer's Saloon. Here's your house."

"That doesn't look like me."

"Of course not," she said, pointing to the key. "This means *boy*."

Ike studied the map. Maybe he needed a

key on his map. "Is this the levee?" he asked, tracing his finger along the river's edge until he found the spot where he'd seen the men on horses. And Mary. "There are trees here," he said, "and lots of brush."

"I'll add that next time. Rematch?" She rolled up the map and laid out her checkers mat.

"I don't have time," said Ike. He turned the compass, watching *north* stay in one place.

"Just one game," said Albirdie.

"For the compass?"

"For the general's button. What do you have?"

Ike checked his pockets and took out a swirly red marble. "Aggie?"

Albirdie put the general's button back and pulled out another, less ornate button. She unrolled the mat and set up her pieces. When Ike hesitated, she did his side, too. Ike absently slid a man forward.

Albirdie made a quick move. Ike moved another piece and right away she jumped two of his men.

"Concentrate," she said.

Ike thought about Mary in the woods and her boys, David and John. *Quick. Bad aim. Can't keep a secret...* Ike moved another man and Albirdie started to jump it, then put her piece back.

"No." Albirdie put his player in another spot. "Come on, Ike. Don't throw them away. Strategy. Never leave an open space behind your man."

"I know that. I just forgot."

She stopped and looked at him hard. "Are you just letting me win? Because that's not fair."

"No! It's not that. I just, I . . ."

"What?"

Ike leaned close to Albirdie. "I saw a woman in the trees by the river," he whispered. Even though there wasn't anyone else in the church, he felt as if God or one of the angels could hear him and might break into song about it any moment, beckoning Cutts and Simms and the sheriff.

"What woman?" she whispered back. "What trees?"

"A colored woman," he said. He glanced around again. *"Mary,"* he said, looking at Albirdie to see if she understood.

"Mary who?"

"From the poster," he said. *"Runaway from the subscriber, Clark County, Mo."* There. He felt like he'd taken off a stone jacket.

Albirdie rolled the checkers mat up with the pieces inside and spread out her map. "Where?" she asked.

Ike put his finger on the place where the trees and brush should be.

"What did you do?" she asked.

"I—" And suddenly he felt ashamed. *Should* he have done something? What could he have done?

"I didn't do anything."

"Did you tell anyone? Besides me?"

"No."

"Well, then you did something. That's good," she said. She rolled up her map and stood.

Ike let out a long breath. He did feel better. He lay back on the pew. Albirdie wasn't a priss, and he regretted saying so to Milton and Morris. He would miss Albirdie.

"Aren't you coming?" said Albirdie. Ike sat up. She was at the door, waiting.

Ike clutched the compass in his hand and followed.

Posters

Downtown, Mr. Douglas from Public Works was trying out his new road scraper, and clumps of people were following its progress, watching the rough dirt street smooth out as he passed.

"Never mind that, Ike. Come on!"

"Where are we going?"

"There's one—stop!" It was a poster of Mary. Albirdie grabbed the lower edge and yanked it off the nail.

"Here," she said, handing it to Ike. "There's another." She crossed the street. Ike slipped the compass in his pocket, folded the paper quickly, and stuffed it inside his shirt, looking around for Mr. Cutts and Mr. Simms.

She was back and handed him a second sheet.

"Someone might see!" said Ike.

"So?"

"Isn't it stealing?"

"No. It's a free country. For some of us."

Albirdie strode down the street toward the post office, and Ike lagged behind.

"Why can't we just leave them?" Ike asked. "This one isn't even about Mary and her boys."

"It's for the war," she said.

"The war is in the South, and I'm going to —" Ike caught himself.

Albirdie stopped and looked at him. "You're going to what?"

"Nothing."

Albirdie studied his face a moment, then continued. "What about Mary and her boys? We can't stay a union while the South still has slaves."

"But we don't have slaves. Negro people are free here. Mr. Jenkins, for instance."

"Not if they are still legally someone's slaves," said Albirdie. She waved the poster. "Mary's not free. Her boys are not free. If Mary or her boys get caught, they are sent back. They have to travel all the way to Canada to be sure they won't be taken back."

"Canada."

Ike took the poster from her. He read the description again, felt Mary's hand on his arm. He folded the paper and tucked it in his shirt with the other one.

They went into the post office. There were notices there as well. One was seeking the infamous Sisters Brothers. They looked dangerous. Mary was not dangerous. Her boys were eleven and seven. How dangerous could they be? He looked at Albirdie. Could they take this poster down with the clerk staring at them from behind the desk?

"Go on and mail your letter, Ike. I'll wait," Albirdie said loudly in an unusually sweet voice. She smiled at the clerk.

"But I don't . . . Oh, I mean, yes. I'm going to mail a letter."

Ike stepped up to the counter.

"Um, how long will it take to get to, um, Hannibal?"

"Can't say. This is wartime, son. Now, do you want to mail something or not?"

Ike dug in his pocket, reached under the compass, and pulled out a marble.

"Shoot," he said. "Forgot my money. All I got's this aggie."

"We only take Iowa money," said the clerk. "Also Minnesota and Wisconsin."

"I guess I'll come back," Ike said, turning and walking out the door as slowly as he could manage. Then he ran to Albirdie, who held up the poster triumphantly.

"We did it!" Ike said.

"Did what?"

Milton and Morris. Morris grabbed the poster and handed it to Milton. "What are you doing here, Ike? Did you get the you-know-what? Is the map done?"

"Map?" said Albirdie. "What map, Ike? Give me that poster, Milton."

"We have business with Ike, Albirdie." Milton handed the poster to Albirdie indifferently, and he started to walk away with Morris close behind. "Aren't you coming, Ike?"

Ike stood between Albirdie and Milton and Morris. Mr. Day was sweeping the boards of the sidewalk. He leaned on the broomstick and watched them.

"They're rats, Ike," Albirdie said. "Ignore them."

"They're rats, Ike," Morris mimicked.

Albirdie stalked off, and though Ike called out, "Wait, Albirdie!" he didn't make a move to follow.

"Wait, Albirdie!" Milton mimicked.

"We're ready, Ike," said Morris. They walked away, but Ike didn't follow them, either.

"Hinmans," scoffed Mr. Day. He returned to his sweeping. Ike took out the compass and turned until it pointed *south,* then he started after Milton and Morris.

Stars and Stripes

Ike ducked into his house and found himself smack in the middle of a room full of women, locked in stony silence. The only sound was the small *pop* as needles poked through red, white, and blue fabric, followed by the small *hiss* as the thread pulled through. Then *pop hiss, pop hiss* as many hands worked on one large flag. He backed away but his mother stopped him.

"Ike, please bring Mrs. Hinman a glass of water. She needs to cool down."

Ike started for the door.

"No, Ike," commanded Mrs. Hinman. "I am perfectly cool, but your mother is too kind. *Too* kind. She'd like to see everyone live in pleasant harmony. *Everyone.*" She looked around the room significantly.

"Now, Myrtle," Mrs. Gorman chided.

"These stars and stripes celebrate our freedom," said Mrs. Hinman. "Our freedom to do as we please. *That's* what our boys are out there fighting for."

Ike's mother stabbed her needle into the flag and stood up.

"I agree, Mrs. Hinman. This flag does stand for freedom. Freedom for *every* person."

"Freedom for our Iowa men to have Iowa jobs," said Mrs. Hinman. "Your freedom for *every* person, *Olive,* means jobs taken up by *other people.* Does that sound like freedom to you, ladies?"

"Now, now," said Mrs. Gorman. "We are here for our soldiers."

"That's *right,*" said Mrs. Hinman. "This is a Soldiers' Aid Society, Olive, not a

Coloreds' Aid Society. I would appreciate it if you would leave all further politicizing out of our meetings."

Ike slipped up to his old bedroom and grabbed the map, then ran down the stairs and over to his pantry room before the women could stop him.

He spread out a kerchief on his cot and put the compass on it. Then he hung it around his neck, tucking it into his shirt. He laid his leaving collection on the kerchief. Slingshot, arrowhead, Lincoln, marbles. It didn't look like enough. What about food?

But before he could put anything away, there were footsteps on the porch, and Albirdie was stepping into the kitchen, then into his room uninvited, closing the door behind her. He put his hand on the lump the compass made under his shirt. For the first time, he felt awkward with Albirdie. He saw her as Milton and Morris saw her. Why didn't she have girl friends? Study to be a nurse like Susannah, or play paper dolls like Jane and LouLou?

"Milton and Morris have you talked into one of their schemes, haven't they?" said Albirdie. "My compass is missing."

"No, they haven't," he said. And it was true. It wasn't their scheme. It was his.

"So this is your map."

She picked up the map and Ike snatched it back from her, tearing a corner.

"Albirdie! See what you did?"

"What *I* did?"

Ike smoothed out the map on his cot.

"Forget it," she said. "It doesn't matter. I need you to come to the church."

"I'm pretty busy," said Ike.

LouLou and Jane pounded on the door.

"Ike, we can't talk here," Albirdie said. "Just come to the church."

They stood there, silent.

"Will you come?"

"Later. I have to do something first."

"It's urgent."

154

"I said I'd come," said Ike. "When I'm done."

Albirdie studied his collection and looked around the small room.

Ike went back to sorting. He straightened the shells. When he turned, she was gone and the compass was still pressed against his chest.

Ready

Morris and Milton were sitting on the roof of the lean-to when Ike came out. Barfoot was pawing the ground with his ears laid back. The boys laughed at him, hopping down when they saw Ike.

"Your horse is so old he should be glue," Milton said.

"One horse for all three families?" said Morris. "Look at him. He's a grandpa."

Ike saw how homely Barfoot really was. That his back dipped like an old mattress. That his coat was dull, despite all of Ike's brushing.

"Leave him alone," he said weakly.

Ike climbed up on Barfoot's back. "Let's go."

"We aren't taking Barfoot to Hannibal," Morris informed him, after a pause.

"I know." Ike slid off Barfoot's back.

"Do you have the map?" asked Milton.

Despite a few smudges and missing details, Ike was proud of his effort, and he held it up for inspection.

Milton handled it roughly. He coughed and used the map to cover his mouth. A bit of spittle landed on Hannibal.

Ike cringed. He moved reflexively to scratch Barfoot's neck, but then backed away and put his hands in his pockets.

"Did you bring drumsticks?" Ike asked.

"That and more," said Milton, holding up a lumpy sack.

Morris took the map from Milton, folding it carelessly and stuffing it in his pocket. "Come on, boys. Ma's going to be at your house for a while now. We told her we're going for a picnic. So we've got plenty of food and she won't be expecting us back for hours."

Ike walked between them. They were the same age but had a long-legged pace that kept Ike rushed and out of step. "Good," he said loudly. "We're going!"

Milton worked up some saliva in his mouth and spit on the road in front of them. "Bet you can't spit that far, Ike."

Ike pushed the back of his tongue against the roof of his mouth and tried to gather a wad of spit, but his mouth was parched.

"I could use some water first," he said. "Did you bring a canteen?"

"Thought you would," said Morris.

"Never mind," Ike mumbled. "There's plenty of water in the river."

They were leaving. They were going out on the river in a boat. They would get to Hannibal and find the men. This was the moment when a man should whistle, care-free and bold, but Ike's mouth was too dry.

The River

Ike pulled the compass from his shirt, and held it up. "Ninth goes northeast. Isn't the levee southeast?" he said. "Shouldn't we be turning down Fulton or going back to Morgan or High?"

"Whichever," said Milton, striding ahead. "The boat's not at the levee. We're going the right way. You'll see."

Morris stopped. "The compass! You got it! Well, Ike Button is not such a disappointment after all," he said. He grabbed for the compass, but Ike pulled it close and stuck it in his pocket.

"Isn't *he* the captain?" said Milton, taking a left on Grand, next to the river.

"We should have gone right," Ike mumbled. But he walked with them along Grand, past stone mansions, then down the grassy riverbank until there were no more houses.

It was wide and flat here, with a bluff rising behind them and another across the river. They slowed, and the boys poked along thick reeds at the river's edge.

"Where is it?" Milton asked.

"It's here," said Morris. "Quit pestering me."

"Quit pestering *me*," said Milton, giving Morris a shove. Morris lost his footing and fell into the moving water. He struggled out and lunged at Milton, but just then Ike spotted something.

"There!" he said. "Is that what we're looking for?"

"Didn't I tell you?" said Morris,

whapping Milton on the head. "Didn't I tell you it would be here?"

There was a small skiff in the under-brush. It was well-worn, with two oars crossing a narrow plank seat.

"Does it float?" Ike asked.

"'Course it floats," said Milton. "It floats, doesn't it, Morris?"

"Sure it *floats.* It's a boat," said Morris.

They stood over it without laying a hand on it. Finally, Morris tossed his picnic sack into the boat. "Who knows when Pa is going to be back," he said to Ike. "We're men of action."

"Yes," said Ike. Exactly. At last. No matter if it lacked the glamour of the *Jeannie Deans,* it wasn't a raft, and they only had to get to Hannibal.

Milton gave the boat a push. "It's not going to bite, boys. Let's get it in the water. Push!"

Ike and Morris took the sides and pushed as Milton stepped into the shallows and pulled. When the stern reached the water and just the prow rested on the sand, they paused, panting.

"Whose boat is it?" Ike asked.

"Mr. . . ." Milton started, but Morris interrupted him.

"It's our boat, Ike. Just give me your sack and hand me that compass and help me get the rest of it in the water."

The skiff was a heavy, flat-bottomed thing. It was as if the boards had soaked up the whole river and weighted it down. Ike placed his sack under the bow.

"The compass," said Morris, holding out his hand.

Ike hesitated. He looked at the face of the compass. *East.*

"It can't get wet," he said. "I'll hold it."

Milton reached for it, but Morris pushed him at the boat. "Let's get this thing in the water," he said.

They edged the prow in. The current

tugged, and Ike held tight to the side, anchoring his feet in the muck.

"I'm going to take the oars first," said Milton.

"I'm the oldest, so I will take the oars first," said Morris.

"The current will take us downriver pretty fast," said Ike. "We won't have to row for a while."

"Exactly," said Morris, and he climbed into the boat and sat squarely on the seat.

"Hold it steady, Ike," said Milton. He tumbled in and knelt on the floor of the boat directly behind Morris.

"OK, Ike. Just push us out a little farther to clear the bottom."

"But how will I get in?"

"Here, hand me the compass," said Morris. "Then I'll help you in."

Ike gave Morris the compass, then reached out for his hand.

"Just give another push first," Milton snapped.

Ike grasped the side, gliding the boat out another foot, then let go to reach for Morris's hand. But Morris swatted him away.

"Sorry, Ike," said Morris.

"It was a great idea," called Milton. "We owe you one!"

"Wait!" Ike cried. He grabbed for the prow but the boat spun sharply out of reach.

Milton and Morris fumbled for the oars. They each took one and dipped them, rowing clumsily.

"No!" Ike screamed. He waded to shore and ran alongside. "Come back! Wait!"

"Tell our mother not to worry!" Milton called.

The brothers argued over the oars, rocking the boat. The current caught them, and they were moving fast. Ike reached for the slingshot still in his waistband, grabbed a stone, and quickly shot it after them, but it was too big and just plopped in the water right in front of him.

"Danged piece of junk!" He tried breaking the slingshot over his knee, then threw it into the brush.

"You'll be sorry!" he hollered, but they could no longer hear him. Their heads were dots; the boat was a small line, dwarfed by a steamboat coming upriver.

Ike raged, pulling a handful of leaves off a low-hanging branch and throwing them into the air, picking up a stick and whacking at the bushes. He yelled and screamed until his lungs were raw, then he dropped down on the sand, his forehead on the grainy pebbles, and cried. He pounded the sand with his fists and heaved big choking sobs until his chest burned.

There was a rustling in the brush. A whinny. Ike rolled over and looked up into Barfoot's snorting face.

"Go away!" Ike said, rising to his knees. But Barfoot leaned his head down and butted Ike's chest, then laid his nose on Ike's shoulder.

Ike swatted at him. "Go on, Barfoot! I don't want you here." He stomped down the shore, but Barfoot followed.

Ike picked up a fistful of sand and flung it at Barfoot. "Can't you see I don't want you here!" Barfoot backed up.

"Barfoot." Ike turned away, willing himself to look at the water only, the river that had taken everything away from him — his brothers, his father, his uncles, his compass, his chance to live up to the family promise that had died with Palmer. When he finally turned his head, Barfoot was gone.

Ike lay flat on the sand and turned his face toward the water lapping the shore. The setting sun was spreading itself over the ripples. He reached out a hand and let pink water lap over it, feeling his stomach press into the sand with each lengthening breath.

As dusk settled, he pulled himself to sitting, hugging his knees close, and rested his chin on his arm. He watched a mosquito hover, then land on his sinewy forearm; watched as it sank its stinger into his arm, relishing the small prick of pain as it took a quick drink, its belly swelling; watched dispassionately as a small bump formed in the spot. He sat on the shore until bats swooped and chattered above him, dipping and diving over the river.

When pink had faded to gray, and then black, and the stars came out, he stood, poked around the brush until he found his slingshot, and picked his way back to the spot where they'd found the boat, tracing the path they'd beaten through the brush. Barfoot was there by the street, standing at attention, regal despite his dipping back and wide belly. Ike reached out and touched his warm side. He climbed up on Barfoot's back.

"Let's go home, Old Pokey," he said.

Home Again

It was long dark when Ike and Barfoot returned. All the mothers and little girls were in the yard, candles flickering on the table. Mrs. Hinman was there, too, with Old Man Hinman.

"There he is!" LouLou called as Ike approached. She and Jane ran to Ike and grabbed his arm as he slid off Barfoot's back, pulling him toward the others. Goldenrod and Marigold leaped up, barking.

Aunt Betsy wept freely. "You're home. Our dear boy is home. Oh, we were so worried." She locked Ike in an embrace.

His own mother wiped her tears quickly and wrestled him away from Aunt Betsy for her own hug.

"You had us worried to ashes, Isaac," said Aunt Sue. She swatted the back of his head, then held him in a stiff hug. "OK, everyone. Party's over. Go on inside. And now we've got Susannah out looking for him. Will the worry ever end?"

"Where are *my* boys?" Mrs. Hinman wailed. "*My* boys have not returned. They're always punctual, my boys. *We'll be home by dark, Ma,* they said, and I sent them with plenty of victuals to last until dark. A picnic. *A picnic,* they said. But what kind of picnic lasts until"—she paused to take a breath and look up at the sky—"lasts until comets cross the sky. Where are my boys, Isaac Button?"

Everyone looked at the sky and then at Ike.

"Isaac?" said his mother. She never called him Isaac.

"I . . . They . . ."

"Where were you, Ike?" Susannah was back. "I looked everywhere."

"He's home now is all that matters," said Aunt Betsy firmly, the soft corners gone out of her voice. "Ike?"

Ike shivered. He wanted to go to bed. His own bed. If his brothers had taken him along in the first place, he wouldn't be in this mess now.

"They're in a boat," he said.

"A boat!" Mrs. Hinman cried. "Isaac Button, what have you done to my boys?"

Ike's mother stepped in front of him. "Myrtle, Ike has not *done* anything to your boys. They find trouble enough without his assistance. Now, if you will address my son politely, I'm sure he'll tell us their whereabouts." She turned to Ike. "Won't you, Isaac?"

Ike gave a brief version of their story, leaving out the part about the unseaworthiness of the boat and the fact that it was his idea. "But it wasn't on purpose. They're probably just camping out at Mud Island," he said.

"Not on purpose?" Mrs. Hinman said incredulously. "No. This is the Button men all over again. Just like that ne'er-do-well Palmer you all pinned your hopes on, with his wild ideas and disastrous outcome. This one has filled my boys with wild ideas. Captain Hinman has preached grace on your debts, but no longer. We're calling them in." She shook her head at Ike and took Old Man Hinman by the arm and led him across the alley. Aunt Betsy shooed everyone into their houses.

Ike went to the pantry. He took the blanket off the bed and went out to the lean-to, where Barfoot was lying down. He took a bale of straw off the stack, broke it apart, and made a nest in the small space next to Barfoot. He spread his blanket on it and lay down, reaching out to rest a hand on Barfoot's side. His insides felt empty, but he wasn't hungry. He closed his eyes and breathed in Barfoot's warm, rhythmic breath.

In the Soup

Ike woke to the sound of sharp voices arguing. He opened his eyes and looked directly up at Barfoot's belly. He wiped sweat off his face. His shirt clung to him. A door slammed. He sat up abruptly, pulling straw from his hair, and listened.

"The moment he's up! The moment he's up!" It was Mrs. Hinman. He ducked down as she crossed the yard at a speed he'd never seen her achieve. When she'd gone, he curled back up in his nest, pulling the blanket over his face.

He breathed the hot straw air. The weight of his losses sat on his chest. Leon,

Jim, his father, Uncle Oscar, Uncle Hugh, Palmer — even though Palmer had already been gone, he seemed more gone now. The bear, Lincoln, a mollusk, the compass. Even the compass.

A hand nudged him, and Ike peered out. Susannah.

"Well, if it isn't our drummer boy. You are in the soup today, Ike. Aunt Betsy's staved Milton and Morris's mother off for now, and your own mother, too, for that matter, but you'd better fortify." She handed him a jellied biscuit and a peeled boiled egg. "The princes must be retrieved."

"Drummer boy?"

Susannah pulled an envelope and a crumpled paper from her pocket. She held out the paper. "I found this under the rug." Ike ate the egg in two bites, then fed the biscuit to Barfoot and stood next to him, reading.

I have taken up drumming. He reddened.

"I was going to write a different one," he said.

"They wrote to us again, but it's only what we already know from the newspaper and Mrs. Gorman. Kate got a private note from Leon, very sentimental. She let me read it." Susannah handed Ike the family letter.

Dear Family,

The crops in Missouri are very fine. So far the mosquitoes are worse than the enemy. Life has gotten dull with none of your fair faces to delight us.

Ike stopped reading. They'd done more than fight mosquitoes. He wished he'd written. He imagined Leon and Jim walking next to General Lyon.

General Lyon would compliment his brothers on their steady nerves in the face of murderous fire. His father would be there, too. Ike was sure that the general could not have a mustache half as fine as his own father's, nor a laugh as hearty.

Or would they be walking? He thought of the one-legged veteran at the Ellis Hotel. What if they'd been in another battle? What if they were lying hurt in a hospital, or on a battlefield? They could have gotten lost since this letter was written. Been captured by rebels.

Susannah interrupted Ike's reverie.

"Albirdie was here looking for you, too, and I've got news from Kate."

Albirdie. He'd forgotten about Albirdie.

"I'm going to help at the hospital. Not as a nurse, but I'll help and learn. I'm going to start tomorrow. Kate says they'll keep us busy day and night. Day *and* night. And word is, they're going to let women muster as nurses soon. Forty cents a day, plus rations. Maybe I'll go. Too bad you're not a girl."

Goldenrod and Marigold took up a furious barking just then and Ike flinched.

"Hang tight, Daddy!" they heard Mrs. Hinman holler over the dogs. "I've waited long enough. I'm going to fetch that Button scoundrel."

"Run!" said Susannah. "I'll distract her."

Battlefield

Ike ran down the alley, crossed the street, and continued down the next alley.

"Hold up, there!" Mr. Box called as Ike passed. "Come help me, will you?"

Ike looked over his shoulder, then ducked into the yard, panting. Mr. Box was holding a bat house up to a fence board near his chicken coop.

"Go pump yourself a drink of water, then hold this nail steady for me, will you?"

Ike cranked the pump lever, leaned over and slurped some, then stuck his whole head under the faucet. He cupped his hands under the water and splashed his shirt.

"Don't drain the whole Mississippi, now," said Mr. Box.

Ike let the end of the stream dribble onto his feet, then he took his place by the chicken coop.

"Your men fighting the good fight, then?" Mr. Box continued, poising his hammer over the nail and Ike's hand.

"Yes," Ike squeaked. He turned his head, unable to watch.

Whack! Mr. Box hit the nail true. Ike stepped back.

"There," said Mr. Box, admiring their work. "That wasn't so bad, was it?"

Ike shook his head.

"Suppose you'd rather be south with the men than here with the likes of this old coot."

"Yes."

"Me too. I suppose there's the same number of women as there were before, but now that so many men are gone, I feel the presence of them all the more, and it weighs on me. Before long, besides the women, it'll be just you youngers, us olders, and the traitors left."

"And all the new soldiers coming to town."

"Well, yes. Them too. Lest Lincoln can wrap up this conflict soon. And he'd better. How are we going to get a crop this year? All the farms emptying out. Men joining up. My own sons left a perfectly fine acreage up by Goodhue. No wives to run it while they're away. Come run our farm, they say. But what's an old man like me going to do with a farm? Just going to let it go fallow, they are, lest Lincoln can dust up this mess."

"Yes," said Ike. "I mean, no. I mean . . ." He shrugged.

"Where are my manners?" said Mr. Box. He went into the house and came out with a bowl of strawberries. "Tewksbury's finest. Sit. Eat."

Ike sat across from Mr. Box and ate strawberries one by one, making a small pile of green stems while Mr. Box continued to talk about his sons and their Goodhue farm and the need. "*You want to find someone to take over, be my everlasting guest,* Waldo says to me. As if it's as easy as all that, persuading someone from a metropolis such as Keokuk to move to a mere hamlet to do my son's work for him." When the last strawberry had been eaten, he nodded and said, "Good. Good. Now, how 'bout a game of chess? You play?"

"No."

"You a checkers man, are you?"

"Yes."

"Either you haven't got much of a vocabulary, or you're afraid of me like all the rest of the ninnies 'round here.

"No matter," said Mr. Box. "I appreciate your help. Get on, then. And come over should you want to learn the fine game of chess. A battlefield on a board, it is. A battlefield on a board."

Mr. Box walked him to the alley. Ike glanced toward his block. No sign of Mrs. Hinman or anyone else looking for him.

He ran through the alleys to the church. He opened the door and let his eyes adjust to the dimness inside.

Albirdie's head popped up from the back pew. "Go away."

"Susannah said you were looking for me. I forgot to come over yesterday. I'm sorry."

"You *forgot*?" Her head disappeared again.

Ike walked up to the back pew. She was lying on her stomach, working on her map.

"Milton and Morris will be in Hannibal by now," she said, not looking up.

"Who told?"

"Susannah. Do you have my compass?"

"No. I . . . They . . ."

"Ike!" She dropped her pencil and stood to face him.

"I'm sorry. They took it." He slid into the

pew and pulled her map toward him. It was good. The woods were there now. She sat down and crossed her arms.

"Susannah said you were looking for me," Ike said.

"I needed your help, but you're too busy trying to get away from here."

"You could have asked Susannah. Or Junior."

"No, Ike. I needed *you*. You're good at solving things. Like in checkers strategy. And it's something I can't do alone. But you have new friends now."

"Milton and Morris aren't my friends." Ike was taken aback. *Good at solving things? Strategy?* Ike sat up taller.

"What happened?"

Albirdie looked around at the empty sanctuary. They could hear her father practicing his sermon in his office.

"Mr. Jenkins was here yesterday when I came back with the posters."

"So?"

"My father was out, so Mr. Jenkins asked me to give him this note." Albirdie held out a folded, sealed paper.

"Did you?"

"No. The sheriff came in when Mr. Jenkins left. He asked for my father, too. Tried to ask me what my father's dealings were with Mr. Jenkins. What if my father does get arrested, like Milton and Morris said?"

"Milton and Morris are rats. You said so yourself. Did you read the note?"

She nodded and held it out for Ike to read.

Dear Sir,

By tomorrow morning's mail, you will receive two small volumes of The Irrepressible Conflict, *bound in black. After perusal, please forward, and oblige. Yours truly,*

J.M.J.

"Books?" said Ike. "What's so important about books?"

"I went to the bookstore but Mr. Ogden says he's never heard of it. I don't think it's about books, Ike."

"Then what?"

"Mary's boys. I just know it. *Two small volumes . . .*"

They studied both sides of the paper and read it again.

"You met Mary. You know where she was. What do we do about her boys?"

"Should we tell your father?"

She shook her head. "Mr. Cutts and Mr. Simms have been lurking around. They are eager for the reward money and are already suspicious of my father."

"So what should we do?"

"They won't suspect children."

"We aren't *children.*"

"To them we are. We're invisible."

Ike read the note out loud.

"It's dated June twenty-sixth. Tomorrow

is today," said Albirdie. "The boys arrive today. Or they're already here. We need to find them and get them to Mr. Jenkins."

"Maybe they are in the same place I found Mary. Let's look at your map."

Ike traced a line along the river with his finger. "There," he said. She handed him a pencil, and he circled a small grove of trees. They read the note again.

"Please forward," Albirdie read. "But how?"

"So we need to get them to Mr. Jenkins," mused Ike. "Remember when we saw Milton and Morris heading downtown in the back of that cart? We'll bring Barfoot and his cart. But I can't go home. Mrs. Hinman is looking for me."

"I'll go fetch them," said Albirdie.

"Good. If anyone at my house asks, tell them it's for the church. I'll go find David and John."

Albirdie nodded.

"Meet me here," Ike said. He drew an X where he'd passed the men on tall horses. "There's a blanket on the straw next to Barfoot. Bring that, too. Whistle to let me know you're there."

Out of Sight

Ike paused at the levee and let the activity swirl around him. Two boats were docked, the *Eagle* and the *Menominee*. The *Eagle* was full of kitchen stoves, which were being unloaded into wagons. It took a half dozen men to lift and transfer each one. Soldiers inspected the decks of the *Menominee*. It was the largest steamer Ike had ever seen. A grand lady stepped off it and swished past him in a wide crimson Southern gown. Crimson! On a Thursday afternoon!

Ike followed the riverbank, trying to remember the spot where he'd gone into the woods before he saw Mary. It was quite a ways, and he broke into a run. Just down the shore, a skiff like the one Milton and Morris had taken was pushing off, moving slowly away. A man in a wide-brimmed hat faced Ike as he rowed, whistling like an owl. Beyond, a steamer puffed into view, and the skiff grew smaller as the steamer grew larger. Ike fought off the familiar sting of disappointment at being in Keokuk.

He looked back toward the levee for Albirdie and Barfoot, but it was too soon for his slow horse to have brought them. He paused, recognizing the spot where he'd seen the men on horses. He'd thrown a stone. He stood at the edge of the brambles. *Two volumes . . . bound in black.* If he did find the boys, then what? Surely, panning for gold was easier than this.

Ike ducked into the brush, trying to re-create the path he'd taken before.

"Hello," he called weakly, hoping for no reply. He paused. This was not the kind of adventure he'd wanted. He would go back to Albirdie and tell her he'd tried. It was no different from missing the *Jeannie Deans*, or from losing Milton and Morris. One quick walk through the woods and he could relieve himself of this duty. He could go back to Barfoot and his nest of straw and could sulk in peace. *I needed your help. Good at strategy.*

Just a few more steps and then he'd turn around. He whistled softly as he walked, but stopped abruptly. A rustle? He stepped around a tree, expecting to see . . . to find . . . but it was just a man relieving himself.

"Scoundrel! Get on!" the man bellowed. "Can't a man make water in peace?"

Ike's nerves released and he laughed. Mary's boys weren't here. He had tried. He would go home now and do any chore Aunt Betsy asked. He'd polish the stove. Scour the floor. Write to his brothers. He'd even face Mrs. Hinman.

He kicked a stone and whooped and hollered and turned to take a shortcut, and came face-to-face with a boy, a colored boy, holding a fat stick, feet spread wide.

"Turn around," the boy commanded quietly. "Put your hands up. You saw nothing."

Ike turned, but not before glimpsing a smaller boy behind this one. He could run now, and no one would be the wiser. He thought about what Mary had said about her boys . . . something about sweets and silver.

These boys did not look sweet.

Ike raised his hands and took a step.

"Keep moving," the boy threatened, his voice cold and hard.

Ike took another step. He wanted to deck him. Here Ike was trying to help, and this was the thanks he got? Maybe these weren't even Mary's boys.

Ike stood still. "David?" he said. "John?"

The stick jabbed into his back again.

"Ow! Stop that!"

"Don't hurt him, Davey!" cried a small voice.

"There's no David or John here," said the older boy.

"I'm Johnny," said the younger boy.

"Quiet!" said the older boy in a low voice. "Who was the man you were with?" He pressed the stick harder against Ike's back, then released it.

"No one. It was just a fisherman or something."

The boy prodded him again. "Why should I believe you?"

Ike paused, scrambling for something to say. "Have you read *The Irrepressible Conflict*?" The question sounded absurd when Ike said it out loud. They hadn't read it at his school. But the coloreds had their own school. Maybe they read different books.

"No," said the boy, but the pressure released from Ike's back and he turned around.

Ike looked into his captor's face. They were the same height. This boy's shirt was faded red, streaked with dirt, and torn. His feet were bare. The legs of his pants were soaking wet. The boy held the stick out, marking the space between them.

"Are you Mary's sons?" Ike asked.

The younger boy limped toward Ike, but David held up his free hand. "Stop, Johnny." He thrust the stick at Ike again. "How do you know her name? How do you know our names?"

Ike looked at the younger boy's foot. It was swollen and red. He glanced behind him, nervous now that the fisherman or someone else would find them. Ike reached slowly into his pocket and removed the note. He tried to give it to David, but David held the stick, unwavering.

"Read it out loud," he said.

Ike read the note and looked up.

"Drop it on the ground and step back." David snatched up the note and put it in his pocket. "What else do you know?"

"Are you going to keep pointing that stick at me?"

"I'll put it down, but keep your distance. If you so much as raise your voice . . ." He slashed the stick in the air, then lowered it.

Ike told about meeting their mother and about Albirdie and the posters and the Reverend and the note and about Mr. Cutts and the bounty hunters.

"Where's our mother now?" said David. "Can you take us to her?"

"I don't know where she is. I thought she might still be here," said Ike. "I'm just supposed to keep you out of sight."

"Until when?" said David.

"Until Albirdie gives the signal," said Ike.

They stood, listening to the rustle of the wind through the trees and the far-off whistle of the steamboat coming upriver.

"Were you on that skiff?" Ike asked. "I saw a man rowing away. Your pants are wet."

David shook his head, but Johnny piped up. "Yes," he said. "And I was scared. It was rocking, and I had to stay way in the bottom."

"Hush," said David.

"Stop hushing me," Johnny said. He scowled at David and turned to face the other way. "Maybe I'll go on without you."

"Don't you ever say that," said David. "Brothers stay together. Don't you *ever* say that again. Why do you think we crossed that river anyhow?" Johnny took a step farther, then sat down, still facing away from them.

"I just want to go home," he said.

"You're home right now, wherever you are with me," David said. "Hear me?"

Ike slumped, suddenly envious of David and Johnny. Leon and Jim had no such notions. Palmer didn't either.

"I want Mama," Johnny whimpered.

"This person in the note, J.M.J.," Ike said. "I think he can help us find your mother."

A warbling whistle came through the trees, then another.

"Albirdie!" said Ike.

Johnny sprang up and grabbed Ike's

hand. David pulled him away, turning to Ike. "We've made it this far on our own. Why should I trust you? How do I know this isn't a trap?"

Ike's anger boiled over. "You don't. You don't know. You can trust me or not. But now there's a boat coming. Soon there will be lots of people to get past, and my friend Albirdie is out there. And my horse. I'm going with them."

He stomped through the trees and found Albirdie right where she said she'd be, with Barfoot pulling the wobbly cart.

"Barfoot!" Ike said. He stroked Barfoot's face, then walked around to inspect the cart. Albirdie had put a straw bale in the back, and the blanket.

"Did you find them?" she asked.

"Yes, but I don't think they'll come with us. I tried. Let's go."

The steamboat sounded again, its tall stacks like dark giants. Ike reached for

Albirdie to help him up on Barfoot's back, but she pointed instead, whispering, "Look."

David and Johnny stood in the shadows.

Ike climbed in the cart and pulled the bale apart, making a deep nest. He grabbed the blanket and jumped down, then waved David and Johnny over. David and Ike lifted Johnny into the cart, and David climbed in after, taking the blanket and pulling it over them. Ike stood back and studied the effect. The cart had an open back. David's feet poked out, so Ike covered them with straw, then sat on the back of the cart, his feet dangling.

"OK, Albirdie. Let's go."

The cart rolled slowly along the shore, and Ike turned and looked past Barfoot to the levee. A stove had dropped off the end of a wagon. Deckhands were running over to help. The new steamer was just pulling in.

"It's the *Hawkeye State!*" Albirdie

exclaimed. "Captain Hinman's boat! And look, Ike, on the upper deck."

Ike hopped out of the cart and ran ahead to look. "Milton and Morris!" He jumped into the cart and crouched down. "Mrs. Hinman will be here soon if she isn't already. Hurry!"

Main

Ike kept his eyes on the levee and the *Hawk-eye State* as Barfoot pulled them slowly up Main. They stopped in front of Day Bros. "I'll wait here," Albirdie said. "Go tell Mr. Jenkins."

Ike walked stiffly, feeling as if the knowledge of the boys was written on his face. A small dog scampered up and barked at his heels as a trio of women paused at Stern & Co. Clothing House.

"Sweet puppy," they cooed. Ike shooed the puppy and hurried on, stopping in the shade of Ohmer's Saloon's awning. He looked across the street at Mr. Jenkins's barbershop. There were men outside. Two large horses were tied up. The horses looked familiar. The men were leaning against the window, so that Ike couldn't see past them into the shop.

The day he had thrown the rock. The day he'd found Mary. They were the bounty hunters from Missouri. Ike slipped into the narrow passage between buildings and watched them. They put cigarettes up to their mouths. They wouldn't be moving for a while.

Ike ran back to Albirdie and the cart. "See those men outside the shop?" he said softly. "They're the men hunting Mary. I can't talk to Mr. Jenkins."

"We can't stay here," Albirdie said. "We can't take them to the church. Where should we go?"

Ike didn't know which way to go. Uncle Palmer only had to go west. His brothers only had to go south.

Johnny coughed. Ike and Albirdie flinched.

"My house," Ike said. He hopped into the cart and slid back, bumping into David and Johnny. "Go, Barfoot!"

The cart lurched forward, but slowly.

As they passed Cutts & Simms Umbrella, Mr. Cutts hurried out and past them, shouting at the men in front of the barbershop. "I got news! Captain Hinman seed with his long-distance glass the colored boys come off a skiff! We got to get to the river!"

Brothers

As they approached Button Row, Ike hopped off the cart and hurried to Albirdie.

"Hopefully everyone will be in back," he said. "I'll go ahead to make sure. Pull up to the front door of my house, really close."

Ike stepped gingerly onto the front porch. He peered through Aunt Betsy's front window. She was in the kitchen, a baby on her hip. The kitchen door was open and the little girls were running along the back porch like they did. Next door at Aunt Sue's he saw his mother lying on the sofa, a cloth over her face. And through his front window he saw a jumble of empty chairs and the flag pulled tight on a quilt stretcher in the middle of the room.

He opened the door and ran up to his old room and back down. The house was empty. He stood just inside the door, watching as Barfoot pulled the cart up to the porch. "Hurry, hurry," Ike urged quietly.

Albirdie slid off Barfoot and stood behind the cart. She shrugged at Ike. He nodded. She threw back the blanket. David slid past her out of the cart, then put Johnny on his back. He ran into the house and followed Ike up the stairs and into his room.

Ike closed the door and leaned against it, holding a finger up to his mouth.

Johnny whimpered and David set him down.

Ike took a step toward the window. A floorboard creaked and he froze, then he started again, cautiously. Aunt Sue was at the yard table with Susannah. Barfoot wandered into view, pulling the empty cart. No Albirdie.

"Barfoot!" Susannah exclaimed. "You old fool."

"How in Sam Hill did that old nag wander off with the cart?" said Aunt Sue.

"He's a he," Ike whispered as he pulled the window mostly shut.

The room was hot, and with the window closed, it would be stifling.

David set Johnny on the bed and sat next to him.

"This is all yours?" Johnny ventured.

"Mine and my brothers'," Ike said quietly.

Johnny curled up in a ball, one hand on his reddened foot. David rubbed his back. Johnny took a few long shuddering breaths, then fell asleep. David sat upright, staring past Ike.

Ike peered out the window again, then sat on the floor underneath it, watching David.

"You can sleep, too, if you're tired," Ike said.

David shook his head.

Ike glanced outside, then stepped gingerly over to his shelf, where he picked up the picture of the men, set it down, laid his slingshot next to it, and ran his hand along the rest of the empty surface. He opened the door a crack, listened, then closed it and sat on the floor, leaning back. How could David be so perfectly still when Ike's insides were scooting around like river bugs?

"David," he said. "Are you afraid?"

David looked at Ike sharply and shook his head.

Ike picked at the scab on his arm. He picked at the dirt under his fingernails. He watched David.

"Why did you leave where you were?" Ike asked. "Isn't it dangerous?"

"Of course it's dangerous. But staying? We couldn't stay. Our master was going to sell us farther south. Mama heard him say so. Already sent my daddy south."

"Mine is south, too."

"That's different," said David. "Your daddy can come back."

They listened to the little girls sing "Ring Around the Rosy" in the backyard.

"All fall down," David whispered along with them as their squeals erupted.

"What difference does south or farther south make?" Ike asked.

"Farther south . . ."

Johnny rustled.

"I'm not going to say in front of Johnny," said David. "Even if he is sleeping."

"How long have you been traveling?"

David paused. "We left thirteen days ago."

Ike whistled. "That's as long as my brothers have been gone. Where do you sleep?"

"Outside, mostly, in fields, empty barns. We stayed two nights in the cellar of someone's house. It was filled with apples and potatoes. They let us take some when we left, but we ate 'em all."

"How did you get separated from your mother?"

"Was a man said he was helping us. Said we'd be less conspicuous traveling separate for a day. His wife took our mother, and we were supposed to meet again in the morning, but it started to feel like they were really going to turn us in. Me and Johnny, we ran. I hoped our mother did, too. Sometimes it's hard to tell who you can trust. Who you can't. Sometimes you just get a feeling."

They sat for a bit.

"Have you helped before?" David asked.

Like this? "No," said Ike.

"How did you know what to do?"

"I didn't. I don't."

It was hot and Ike's shirt clung to him. When Aunt Betsy called for the girls to go inside, he raised the window again and sat under his shelf, hoping for a breeze to come through.

They sat silently for a long time then. Ike's own eyes drooped. He caught his head as it fell to his chest. He looked up at David, who was still awake, but taking long blinks.

"Who's that?" David asked, pointing above Ike's head.

"The Button men." Ike brought the picture over and sat on the bed next to David. "My dad, Uncle Hugh, Uncle Oscar, Uncle Palmer."

"They all went south?"

"Yes. Well, except Palmer."

"Where's Palmer?"

"California. Well, he *was* there, until he drowned."

"How'd he get to California?"

"It's a long story."

"OK."

Ike lay back on the bed and stared up at the ceiling.

"There were four brothers," Ike began. "Hugh, Oscar, Dan, and the youngest, the greatest of the Buttons, Palmer. He was everyone's favorite. When Palmer told a story, babies laughed and grown men cried.

He could break the wildest horse and go four days without food or water. His favorite food was pie. He'd have eaten skunk if it were baked in a flaky crust."

He looked over. David was smiling.

"What else?" David asked.

"Well, the family was traveling. All together, from Illinois, heading west to find their fortune. I wasn't born, or maybe I was, but I don't remember. The Button brothers and their brides and the first children to be born stopped in Keokuk. It was June, and the strawberries were ripe. There was an establishment on Main that's not there anymore. They made every kind of pie. Strawberry pie, cheese pie, meat pie."

"Skunk pie?"

Ike laughed. "Probably," he said. "So, here was this town with a river and commerce and pie. The family made friends with a river captain."

"Hinman?"

"Mm-hmm."

"They were just going to make Keokuk a stop on their way farther west. But the river captain had them do some work. Various jobs around town, as he had various holdings. And when they were just about to move on, one night, their horses were stolen, every one, and their wagons."

"Did they find them?"

"No," said Ike. "*It's a sign,* they said. *This is where we should stay.* And so they stayed."

"Except Palmer," said David.

"Except Palmer. Palmer got restless. Word came of gold in California. It was everywhere. A fellow could dip his cup in a stream and bring it up filled with glittering gold."

David whistled softly.

"Palmer didn't have a horse, so he found one roaming the street one night."

"Stole it," David interjected.

"No. I don't think he stole it. Borrowed it, maybe, but the point is, he went west. He met up with men who showed him where to find the gold. He sent some back with a Keokuk man once, who'd been out there and was coming back to marry his gal. This man said Palmer had lots more. Lots more. But there was a fight and, well, seems all the gold in his pockets weighed Palmer down, and he drowned."

The boys lay there listening to Johnny breathing.

"Palmer," David scoffed. "You've got it all wrong about Palmer."

Ike sat up. "What do you mean?"

"Your dad, your uncles, they had you and your brothers and sisters and cousins, right?"

"Yes, well, some of us, anyhow. The little girls weren't born yet."

"They got you all lined up in these houses, right?"

"At first just one house, but then, yes."

"So they stuck it out with the family, stayed close, and he just left them all to go off on an adventure?"

"That's not how it was," said Ike. But as he spoke, the place he'd had Palmer in his head shifted. "Palmer was always the one to point everyone in the right direction."

"Sounds like he pointed himself in the right direction and left everyone else to fend for themselves."

"He did send gold. And a carved bear, the symbol of California, which I had and lost. I must have told the story wrong. Palmer's like . . . well, he's like me."

"No, he wasn't," said David. "You are here with Albirdie, and your mom and sisters. And us. Johnny and me. You could be turning us in for a big fat reward, but you didn't. You aren't."

Ike nodded slowly.

"You aren't, right?"

"No!" said Ike. "I'm not."

"OK, then."

David lay down next to Johnny. "I may close my eyes now for just a minute. But I won't be asleep."

"Me too," said Ike. He closed his eyes. "I won't be asleep." He listened to Johnny's deep, nasally breathing, and David's quick, shallow breaths. He thought about Leon and Jim and tried to imagine them here, now. He saw them as they'd been when he was small like Johnny. Jim was carrying Ike on his back. Ike was peering over Jim's shoulder at . . .

"Isaac Button!"

Ike woke with a start. His mother stood in the wide-open door.

David sat up and grabbed Johnny, who cried out.

"Shh!" Ike and David said at once.

Mother stepped into the room and closed the door behind her.

"Isaac!" she said sharply.

"I . . . They . . ."

Ike reached under the bed and pulled out the poster from the day with Albirdie. She skimmed it, then looked at David and Johnny in alarm.

"Is this Albirdie's doing?" she said.

"No," said Ike. "Mine."

They all watched Mother. She furrowed her brow, walked to the window, and came back to stand in front of them. She glanced at the poster again and reached out her hand to David. "David," she said. "Pleased to know you. And John?" Johnny nodded.

Ike told her about Albirdie and the note and Mr. Jenkins.

"I see," she said. She chewed her lip, studying them. "You boys must be hungry."

"Yoo-hoo!" A voice came up the stairs just then. "Olive, are you up there?"

"The Aid Society will be here soon," said Ike's mother. "Hm."

She opened the door. "Be right down!"

She looked out the window and back at Ike and David and Johnny.

"Seems we have a situation on our hands."

The door opened then, and Aunt Sue burst in with Susannah and Aunt Betsy.

"They'll be here any minute, Olive, and —"

"Close the door, Sue," said Ike's mother. The women and Susannah stared.

"Sue, don't gape. Go warm a plate of food. Susannah, bring water and a washrag."

"But I . . ." Sue gasped. "Well, I never."

"Olive's right, Sue," said Aunt Betsy. "Just do what she says. I'll go cancel the meeting."

"Say I'm feeling delicate," said Olive. "The ladies will believe that. Besides, Mrs. Hinman will rather have the time with her prodigal sons than the likes of us. We can't move them until after dark."

"Think we can keep it from the little girls that long? They'll tell everyone they see," said Susannah, returning with the water.

"Right," said Ike's mother. "Sue, don't you have a basket of buttons that need sorting? Set them up at the yard table. That'll buy us a little time."

Aunt Sue and Aunt Betsy scurried out. Susannah knelt by the boys and studied their bruised and cracked feet.

215

Johnny showed her his swollen foot. "I stepped on something I oughtn'ta," he said.

"I know what to do," Susannah said. "Wait here." She came back with her nursing book and dipped a clean rag in the pan of water.

"Now, Ike," said his mother. "Suppose you come downstairs and tell me what's going on."

When Ike returned, David and Johnny were finishing the food Aunt Sue had brought up for them. "What now?" asked David.

"Are we going to see Mama today?" Johnny asked.

"I don't know," said Ike. "I hope so. I think so."

There was a swift knock at the door, and Albirdie came in.

"You'll have to eat quickly," she said. "We're going to have to try to get you to Mr. Jenkins."

"But it's not dark yet," said Ike. "We should wait until dark."

"It's the men from Missouri," she said. "They were at the river with Mr. Cutts. Milton and Morris saw us there with the cart and told, Ike. My father heard and sent me here to warn you. We have to move."

On the Move

David and Johnny huddled on the sofa in fresh clothes while three mothers, Ike, Albirdie, Susannah, and a flock of little girls buzzed around them. The drapes were drawn. Everyone talked in hushed tones. Fresh straw under the carpet rustled with every footfall.

"Susannah," Aunt Betsy ordered. "Pack the boys a picnic lunch. A big one."

"Ike," said Mother. "Give your shoes to David, and find him a pair of socks. Jane, help Johnny put on these hand-me-downs."

Johnny winced as Jane helped him pull a shoe over his swollen foot.

"Let's not tie this one," she said.

"Everyone knows what they are to do?" said Mother.

They all nodded.

"Good. We'd better get started."

Ike and Susannah went to the lean-to and hitched Barfoot to the cart.

Susannah threw in more straw while Ike soothed Barfoot. They led him close to the back porch.

Albirdie kept lookout at the alley, while LouLou and Jane watched around the side of the house. Aunt Sue stood on the porch, holding the babies.

Susannah and Mother climbed onto the bench seat while Ike stood behind the cart, watching the Hinmans' yard for any sign of movement.

Aunt Betsy opened the door. "OK?" she called quietly, David and Johnny just behind her.

"Just a minute," said Ike. He ran up to his room and back down. He handed David the picture of the Button men. "This is the closest I've got to a picture of me." Then he pulled his slingshot from his waistband and two stones from his pocket and stuffed them into David's other hand.

"Mrs. Button!" Albirdie hollered. "They're coming!"

"Let's go, Johnny," said David. "Front door."

"No," said Aunt Betsy, holding him back.

"Wait," said Ike. He dashed out to Albirdie, and together they ran toward the approaching horses. It was Mr. Cutts and Mr. Simms with the Missouri men.

Ike waved his arms to stop them.

"Sirs!" he said, standing in their path. They ignored Ike and simply guided their horses around them.

"Hinman says Buttons are four houses up this alley. We'll find them there," Mr. Simms said as they passed.

"Wait!" Ike yelled. "You've got the wrong house!" They pulled up their horses and turned toward Ike and Albirdie. The men from Missouri had long shotguns across their saddles as well as pistols holstered at their waist. They looked down at Ike, and he froze. Albirdie nudged him.

"He's right!" she said, stalling.

"The Buttons live on the other side," he said, pointing to the Hinman house.

"Thank you, little man," said one of the Missouri men. "Simms, can't you get anything right?" He dug his heels into his horse's flank and veered around Cutts and Simms into the Hinmans' yard.

"But . . ." Mr. Simms began. He swatted a wasp away from his horse's ear. And then another. "Blasted!" he said.

There were wasps everywhere. Mr. Cutts and Mr. Simms spurred their horses, turned in the direction they'd come, and galloped away.

Ike and Albirdie ran to the Button yard. No Barfoot. No cart. The doors and windows of the Button houses were closed.

"Look," Ike said. The wasp nest had a

hole in it. The stone he'd given David was on the ground underneath it. Ike ducked under the hovering wasps to pick it up, then he and Albirdie ran between the houses to the street just as Barfoot trotted around the corner, pulling the cart out of sight.

"Good-bye," Ike whispered.

In the Stars

Clanging bells split the dawn.

Ike snapped awake.

"Leon! Jim!" He thrashed his arms but the wide bed was still empty.

He scrambled to the window. The ringing went on, like a year of Sundays all at once.

Independence Day.

Aunt Betsy, Aunt Sue, and his mother appeared in the yard with robes tied over their nightgowns. They settled at the table with steaming mugs of coffee. As the echo of the bells faded, Ike leaned out to listen.

"It's settled, then?" said Aunt Betsy.

"Mr. Box brought me the letter last night," his mother answered. "House is big enough for us now, and when our men return, some of us can live in the hired hand's cabin."

"Oscar says they'll muster out in August," said Aunt Sue. "We'll have it ship-shape by then."

"Mr. Day will come with his team and wagon, after the parade."

"I've written Daniel," said his mother. "I hope the letter finds them safe."

Then *crack!* A shot rang out in the distance, then another.

Ike tucked his nightshirt into a pair of pants and ran down the stairs and out the back door.

The mothers were standing, hands on hearts, as the little girls ran out, wailing.

Crack, crack, crack.

"Happy Independence Day!" Susannah shouted as the little girls huddled around her.

After breakfast, dishes were cleaned at the pump and layered with linens in boxes. The girls made piles on the porch: clothing, kitchen, sundries. Ike and Susannah heaved the sewing machine table to the lawn.

"Is there news?" he asked for what seemed like the hundredth time over the past three days.

"Here." Susannah held out a folded piece of paper. "Albirdie brought this over after you were asleep last night. It's from David."

It was a drawing. Two boys stood under a starry sky. A tall woman stood next to them.

"Mr. Jenkins told Albirdie they're with their mother," Susannah said. "They are on their way north."

Ike smoothed the paper. A faint line connected some of the stars.

"A bear," he whispered. He refolded the paper and put it in his shirt pocket.

"I'm going to the parade with Kate,"

said Susannah. "Thomas is marching with the City Rifles. There's time. You should go with Albirdie."

Ike found David's discarded shirt. He tore it into strips and tied one on Barfoot's mane and two on his tail.

"There are your stripes, Old Pokey," he said. "Now you look ready for a parade." He climbed on Barfoot's back, then slid off and went into his quiet house. His mother's letter was on the dining-room table. Ike turned it over and picked up her pen.

Dear Leon and Jim,

The war is happening here, too.
Come home safe. Come home soon.
Your brother,

Ike

He tucked it into the envelope and ran out to Barfoot.

"Come on," Ike said. "Let's get Albirdie."

Ike and Albirdie followed the thundering of feet and thumping of drums to Main. Calvary Captain Sample passed, then a small brass band.

"It's Thomas!" said Ike as the rifles marched into view. From their perch atop Barfoot, Ike and Albirdie watched the Home Guards, the Washington Guards, the mayor, the poet of the day, Albirdie's father with the rest of the city clergy, and the judges and lawyers. The civic societies followed, including Mrs. Gorman and Mrs. Hinman, carrying the Aid Society flag.

Then the citizens left the sidewalks and followed, led by a small band.

"My Country, 'Tis of Thee," the piccolo trilled, and everyone broke into song.

Ike and Albirdie joined in, loud and off-key. Barfoot dipped his head and whinnied along.

227

Author's Note

Although Ike is a fictional character, I placed his story in the midst of actual historical events.

Early in 1861, several southern states seceded from the union of the United States, naming Jefferson Davis provisional president of the Confederate states. In March, Abraham Lincoln was inaugurated president of the union, and in April, shots were fired on Fort Sumter, launching the country into a civil war.

North and south, men left their homes and gathered to form armies. Over the course of the war, more than 76,000 of those volunteers came from Iowa.

Iowa was a free state, but the Fugitive Slave Act of 1850 made it illegal to help freedom seekers, people who were escaping slavery. The penalty was a thousand-dollar fine and six months in jail. The Emancipation Proclamation, which freed slaves, would not be signed until 1863. So although there were free blacks living all across Iowa, including in Keokuk, freedom seekers like Mary, David, and Johnny would have been returned to their owners if they were caught.

Scores of freedom seekers did cross into Iowa. Many found their own way north or were assisted by free blacks. Others were sheltered by a loose network of abolitionists known as the Underground Railroad. The true extent of this network is unknown. Because of the necessity for secrecy, very few records were kept and most people kept their assistance secret.

An 1861 article in the Keokuk *Gate City* newspaper describes a shrill and terrifying steamboat whistle breaking into a June night, waking the town and drawing crowds to the levee. The report of the arrival and departure of the steamboat *Jeannie Deans* captured my imagination and launched me into Ike's story.

For the sake of streamlining the narrative, I took liberties with select dates and details, while trying to stay true to the mood and import of the time and place. I merged the experiences common to many towns of the time. The first regiment to leave was actually the Iowa Second, and most of the men from these first companies were from other parts of Iowa. Keokuk men would leave later.

Scores of intriguing details had to be omitted. I encourage readers who want to learn more about the Civil War to go to their local library, as I did, and read the many firsthand accounts and nonfiction books on the subject and explore such websites as www.civilwar.org. Visit historic sites and history museums. And as you do, imagine yourself in the story — or make up a fictional character of your own.

Acknowledgments

I am indebted to librarians far and near for their time, enthusiasm, creative brainstorming, and assistance in gathering materials, including Tonya Boltz and the staff of the Keokuk Public Library; Dina Stansbury, Karen Brown, and the staff at the Monterey Public Library; and Carol Shields at the Seaside branch of the Monterey County Free Libraries.

The people of Keokuk were generous with their time and knowledge, including my host, Julia Logan; researcher Terry Altheide; and the enthusiastic volunteers of the Keokuk Historical Society. Lynn Koos at the African American Museum of Iowa in Cedar Rapids read and shared valuable resources and expertise.

Mighty thanks to those who read and/or gave advice at critical junctures: Dan Baldwin, Jacqueline Briggs Martin, Leigh Brown Perkins, Michelle Edwards, Maria Hanson, and Lauren Stringer.

The support of my California writers group is invaluable. Cheers to Kate Aver Avraham, Carol Diggory Shields, Paul Fleischman, Elin Kelsey, and Jill Wolfson.

I am grateful for the dedication and artfulness of my editor, Deborah Noyes; designer Pam Consolazio; the enthusiasm and keen eye of Miriam Newman at the finish line; and the whole Candlewick team, who turn my words into beautiful books.

Finally, a special thank you to Bryce Hodges, whose well-timed declaration of enthusiasm for a Civil War–era story set my notion into motion.